Writing for Anthology Book 2

Edited by Maria Kinnersley

Co-Authors – Sheila Winckles, Leighton King, Doug Dunn, Linda Corkerton, Ann Turner, Jacqueline Ellis, Brenda Heale, Jean Newman, Arnold Sharpe, Helen Cowell, Trudy Abbott, Michael Dudley, Audrey Cubbold, Peter Debnam, Peter Duxbury, Nolan Clarke, Maria Kinnersley, Jane Shann, Rose White, Roy White, Sarah Sykes and June Weeks

(Members of the BTAT Writing for Enjoyment Group)

D565656 1 900297

Copyright © December 2024 Maria Kinnersley

All rights reserved. Any unauthorised broadcasting, public performance, copying or recording will constitute an infringement of copyright. No part of this book may be reproduced or transmitted in any form or by any means, electronically or mechanical, including photocopying, fax, data transmittal, internet site, recording or any information storage or retrieval system without the express written permission of the publisher except for the use of brief quotations in a book review.

Printed in the United Kingdom

The author can be found at:
maria75.kinnersley@gmail .com

Cover image: Picture by Linda Garrett

ISBN 9798301509711

Published by   BTAT Writing for Enjoyment Group

DEDICATION

This book is dedicated to Arnold Sharpe,
a good friend and encourager. He was
one of the founder members of the BTAT
Writing for Enjoyment Group and was
an inspiration to us all.
Sorely missed.

ACKNOWLEDGMENTS

Thanks to June Weeks, Jane Shann, Peter Debnam and Doug Dunn for their help and encouragement in the producing of this book.

Contents

Introduction 1

Rabbits 2

   Rabbits by Sheila Winckles 3

   Rabbit on the Moon by Doug Dunn 4

   A Rabbit Recipe by Sarah Sykes 6

   Rabbits on the Run by Arnold Sharpe 9

   White Rabbits by Maria Kinnersley 11

Spring 13

   Different Springs by Sheila Winckles 15

   It's Spring by Maria Kinnersley 16

   Spring by Doug Dunn 18

   Spring Cleaning by Sarah Sykes 20

   Spring Again by Brenda Heale 21

   Stepping Out by Arnold Sharpe 23

   Springtime in Iran by Rose White 25

   Spring by Michael Dudley 27

Your Favourite Activity/Pastime 29

   Nature Interest by Peter Duxbury 30

   A Hobby? by Jean Newman 31

   Writing Letters by Brenda Heale 33

My Hobby by Peter Debnam 35

Knitting Socks by Maria Kinnersley 38

An Experience by Leighton King 40

Information 44

Information by Peter Duxbury 45

Information by Maria Kinnersley 46

Family and Friends 49

For Ida by Rose White 50

Relationships by Sheila Winckles 52

My Family by Michael Dudley 54

Family and Friends by Trudy Abbott 55

A Children's Story 57

Night Flight by Leighton King 58

A Creaky Floorboard Jean Newman 60

Childhood by Doug Dunn 65

Oslo by Arnold Sharpe 68

Games 70

Games by Sheila Winckles 71

Playground Games by Brenda Heale 72

Game of Life by Arnold Sharpe 74

Mundane 77

A Mundane Day? by Jean Newman 78
Mundane Day? by Arnold Sharpe 80
Dreamin' the Sink by Peter Duxbury 82
Mundane by Michael Dudley 84
My Cardigan by Sheila Winckles 86
A Mundane Date by Leighton King 88
Autumn by Michael Dudley 91
Must Try Harder by Brenda Heale 92

How To? 94
A Long Flight by Peter Debnam 95
Any Answers? by Arnold Sharpe 97
Staying in Charge by Brenda Heale 99

Eavesdropping 101
Overheard by Jean Newman 102

Gift 105
A Gift by Maria Kinnersley 106
A Short Word? by Peter Duxbury 109
The Gift by Rose White 111
Christmas Gift by Brenda Heale 113
The Best Gift of All by Arnold Sharpe 115

A Winter's Tale 118

Toronto - 1971 by Roy White.................... 119

A Winter's Tale by Brenda Heale.............. 122

A Winter's Tale by Arnold Sharpe 124

Winter Past by Jean Newman 128

A Winter's Tale, Tale by Doug Dunn........ 131

Diary Entry 134

October 16th, 1793 by Brenda Heale......... 135

The Decision Makers by Rose White 136

July 7, 1880 by Jane Shann 139

1st May 1945 by Jean Newman 141

A Battle by Arnold Sharpe 143

Che Guevara - 25th November 1956 by Peter Debnam.. 147

The Witness by Roy White......................... 149

Love Letter.. 153

Dearest pillow .... by Jane Shann.............. 154

Smoothy by Maria Kinnersley..................... 156

Love Letter for Me by Peter Duxbury...... 157

A Coffee Machine by Peter Debnam 159

My Love by Arnold Sharpe 160

My Favourite by Doug Dunn 162

Grumble 164

A Rant or Diatribe by Roy White 165

An Argument by Linda Corkerton 166

Grumble by Brenda Heale 168

A Grumble by Jean Newman 169

Let's Grumble by June Weeks 172

Not a Grumbler? by Arnold Sharpe 172

Mr Grumble by Peter Duxbury 175

Mustn't Grumble by Doug Dunn 176

The Best Holiday 179

Wonderful World by Audrey Cobbold 180

The Best Holiday by Jacquie Ellis 182

Life Holidays by Peter Debnam 183

The Best Holiday by Jean Newman 186

Scilly Islands by June Weeks 189

With Precious Rose by Roy White 191

Best Holiday Ever by Doug Dunn 193

My Best Holiday? by Arnold Sharpe 195

The Best Holiday? by Peter Duxbury 197

Closed Door 200

The Closed Door by Jane Shann 201

The Closed Door by Jean Newman 202

The Closed Door by June Weeks 205

The Closed Door by Peter Duxbury 207

The Closed Door by Trudy Abbott 208

The Closed Door by Sheila Winckles 210

Closed Doors by Doug Dunn 211

A Child's Thoughts by Brenda Heale 213

The Closed Door by Linda Corkerton 214

Something That Scares You 217

A Fearful Moment by Jean Newman 218

My Solo Flight by Leighton King 220

That Scares Me by Jane Shann 225

Fear by Roy White 226

What Do I Fear? By Brenda Heale 228

My Greatest Fear by Jacqueline Ellis 231

What was I Afraid of? by Doug Dunn 232

A Memory by June Weeks 234

Being Cast Adrift by Nolan Clarke 235

Tracey Troopers 238

Tracey Troopers by Helen Cowell 239

Forty 245

The year of 1984 by Linda Corkerton 246

Forty by Brenda Heale 248

Forty Years on by Maria Kinnersley 248

The 'Forties' by Peter Debnam 250

Rainy Days by Ann Turner 251

Forty by Jane Newman 252

Musings on '40' by Jane Shann 254

What Matters 256

Resolutions by Arnold Sharpe 257

What Matters by Peter Debnam 258

All I Want for Christmas… 261

Christmas Memories by June Weeks 262

Christmas Past by Peter Duxbury 263

All I Want… by Brenda Heale 265

What I Wish by Jean Newman 266

Friendship by Maria Kinnersley 267

Christmas by Jacqueline Ellis 270

Introduction

Welcome to the second 'Writing for Pleasure' book. When the writing group started up in 2019, I don't believe any of us thought we would be publishing books or presenting our work to fellow BTAT members.

I'm indebted to those same members who, by their enthusiasm have encouraged us all to produce pieces that inform and entertain.

Although we have grown in numbers, we have also lost some. Sadly, since the last book was published in September 2023, Michael Dudley, Rose White and Arnold Sharpe have died. Nevertheless, their work lives on in this book as part of a selection of pieces written over the past twenty months.

In a change to the format, I have used the titles of the 'suggested exercises' for each section. Some you will have heard in past presentations, but they are all interesting.

So, I invite you to sit back with your favourite tipple, be it tea, hot chocolate or something stronger, and enjoy a pleasurable read.

Writing for Pleasure Book 2

Rabbits

Rabbits by Sheila Winckles

I was surprised to learn that 2023 is the Year of the Rabbit in China. I had never thought of China having little furry rabbits running round! But apparently, they represent hope and bring a year representing longevity and astuteness.

Most people love these animals. It's their size and soft fur which is so appealing especially to children. In stories such as Brer Rabbit and Brer Fox it is the vulnerable rabbit who outwits the cruel tricks of the wicked larger animal.

I remember when I was at school and studying Australia, we were told there were no rabbits in this country until the early nineteenth century when Thomas Austin, a wealthy settler who lived in Victoria, had thirteen European rabbits sent out to him to breed for hunting. Apparently, it took only fifty years for these rabbits to spread across the entire country becoming one of the fastest spreading species in the world. They can have litters four times a year and birth as many as five kits each time.

Rabbits are predicted to be gentle, quiet, elegant and alert as well as quick. One of the most intriguing acts to watch years ago was a conjuror producing a rabbit out of a hat. A gasp would go up from the audience. Now this is not allowed and said to be cruel, but it certainly enthralled the audience.

Years ago, when we lived in Kent our daughter Debbie, an avid animal lover, was given one of these lovely fluffy animals. She named it Ginny after Virginia Wade and Ginny travelled with is to Cambridge when we settled there. We made a large, covered run for Ginny to exercise in when we put her out in the garden. We had Ginny for several years and were saddened when she died.

Talking about Ginny and telling Debbie I was writing about her and rabbits Debbie laughed and said, "Mum Ginny was a guineapig not a rabbit!"

Oh dear!

Rabbit on the Moon by Doug Dunn

In December 2013 the Chinese soft-landed a probe on the surface of the Moon as part of their Chang'e 3 mission. Their objective was to carry out their first roving exploration and develop key technologies for future missions. The lunar rover was called Yutu which literally means Jade Rabbit.

This was the first return to the surface of the Moon since 1976. Though unable to move after the second lunar day, or 14 earth days, Yutu continued to gather useful information until October 2015. It had driven to a distance of 114 metres from the lander.

In 2019 the Chinese sent another rabbit rover to the Moon, Yutu-2, this time to explore the far side of the Moon. Yutu-2 is currently operational making it the longest-lived lunar rover. One of the mission aims was to investigate an unusually shaped boulder dubbed the "Mystery Hut" or "Moon Cube".

In December 2021, after a one-month trip to reach the rock, the "Mystery Hut" was found to actually be irregularly shaped, and to some, it looked a bit like rabbit. This was fitting as the rover's name Yutu means Jade Rabbit.

According to East Asian and indigenous American folklore, the moon contains an image of a mythical rabbit. Based on Pareidolia, a tendency to impose meaning to nebulous visual stimuli, the markings on the moon are interpreted as a rabbit pounding with a mortar and pestle.

In some Asian folklore, a rabbit resolved to practice charity on the day of the full moon. But with only grass to offer, the rabbit threw itself into a fire. But it was not burnt and touched by the rabbit's virtue, a man drew the likeness of the rabbit on the Moon for all to see.

This year 2023, is the Year of the Rabbit according to the Chinese Zodiac. Similar to the Western Zodiac, the Chinese Zodiac is based on 12 animals but changes each year rather than each month. The Chinese New Year started on the 22 January. Why? Because it is based on the lunar calendar and that is the date of the first New Moon of this year.

Happy Chinese New Year everyone!

A Rabbit Recipe by Sarah Sykes

I have known the tiny island of Malta since the nineteen sixties, when it was still a developing country. I had the opportunity of visiting St Luke's Hospital for a month as a medical student. I met and subsequently married a Maltese doctor, and I lived on the island for fifteen years during the nineteen seventies and eighties. It was fascinating to live in a totally different culture. Malta was more Catholic than Rome. The climate was Mediterranean, and the British Navy was still stationed there for part of the time. The friendly Maltese people ate, of course, a Mediterranean Diet, and the favourite dish for Sunday lunch and celebrations was.... Rabbit Stew. I will give you a list of the ingredients, and it was absolutely delicious.

Ingredients

2 rabbits skinned and jointed, with or without liver and kidneys

¾ bottle robust red wine (cheap and cheerful)

approx. 2 wine glasses of water

2 onions, finely chopped

4 garlic cloves, peeled and crushed

8-10 bay leaves

1 x 400g can tomato polpa (pulp) or whole plum tomatoes mashed up

3 tbsps. tomato puree

2 carrots, peeled and sliced

6-8 medium potatoes, peeled and roughly chopped

salt & pepper

3 tbsp regular olive oil

When I first lived in Malta most people started work or school very early in the morning and went home at midday for a home cooked meal and a siesta. Then shops and businesses opened up again from four in the afternoon until seven at night. At midday you could walk down the road and smell the delicious soups and meals being cooked in every home. I learned how to cook Maltese food from my husband's mother, who faithfully cooked every day for her husband and their family of nine children. We were sometimes given a gift of a freshly killed and skinned rabbit, so I needed to know what to do with it.

When I finally left Malta and returned home to the UK in 1991, I was able to keep a tiny farmhouse with an inner courtyard situated in an alley in Naxxar as a holiday home. Behind this house lived an elderly gentleman who told me that he and his wife had brought up a family of eleven children in his house which was even smaller than mine, but which had a piece of land as big as an average English garden behind it.

On this land he kept rabbits and chickens in cages. He had a few lemon and orange trees, and he grew potatoes, onions, cabbage, and herbs such as marjoram, basil and rosemary. Capers and prickly pear and grow wild in Malta. Every village had a bakery which would bake fresh bread two or three times a day. The sea was full of amazing, tasty fish: Lampuki which the Romans used to love, and many other varieties. Can you see where I am taking you? These people were self-sufficient.

Rabbits on the Run by Arnold Sharpe

Run rabbit, run rabbit, run, run, run,
Run rabbit, run rabbit, run, run, run,
Bang, bang, bang, goes the farmers gun,
So run rabbit, run rabbit, run, run, run,

Run rabbit, run rabbit, run, run, run,
Don't give the farmer his fun, fun, fun,
He'll get by without his rabbit pie.
So run rabbit, run rabbit, run, run, run,

As a boy in the 40's we often had rabbit pie. Meat was in short supply and my father would come home from the pub with a rabbit tucked under his arm, neatly wrapped in newspaper. I would watch fascinated as my father cleaned and skinned the animal. I was equally fascinated watching my mother cook it. This was only surpassed by our enjoyment of eating it. Care had to be taken not to break a tooth on a piece of lead shot.

Lots of people, including children, carried a rabbit's foot for good luck. I often wondered why. The rabbit whose foot we had been given hadn't been so lucky so how come he passed his luck on to the carrier?

With meat in short supply, it was a good job that rabbits were prolific breeders otherwise they may well have become extinct before the end of the war.

Then in the 70's along came a book. Watership Down by Richard Adams. A story of rabbits fleeing destruction and seeking a new home and future for themselves. A story of adventure, heroism and skulduggery before their mission could be concluded. I found myself enchanted by Hazel, the leader with his band of colleagues, Fiver, Big Wig and the other members of the escaping party. The many adventures and enemies they encountered along their way culminated in their epic confrontation with the arch villain General Woundwort. Read into the story what you will but the story, for me, remains a classic. The film did not do justice to the book but the song from it, Bright Eyes, lingers on.

Since reading the book eating rabbit, for me, is out of the question. Perhaps with similar stories about cattle, pigs, sheep and poultry I may consider becoming a vegan.

White Rabbits by Maria Kinnersley

Shelley stirred and turned onto her back. She stretched, yawned then…

"White rabbits, white rabbits, white rabbits, on the first of the month," she said, her eyes scrunched up. "Bring me some luck."

Yesterday had not been good. It had begun with a reprimand from her boss for being late.

"I don't want to hear it," he said as she tried to explain the late bus. "This isn't the first time. Continue like this and you won't have a job at all!"

Shelley managed to get through the day. Every time she thought about getting the sack, tears would well up.

After work, she met Len her boyfriend for a date. In the restaurant, she launched into her tale of woe.

"I don't want to hear it," said Len. "You're always grumbling, and I've had a tough day too."

At that, Shelley's eyes filled with tears. Ignoring his pleas for her to stay, she fled and made her way home by bus.

She arrived home and spent the evening in her bedroom hungry and ignoring the repeated beeps from her mobile.

"Well, today is a new day," she muttered, in the morning as she prepared for the day ahead.

When she arrived home in the evening, she couldn't stop smiling. The boss had been kind and apologised for his tough words. Len had sent a bouquet of flowers and a box of chocolates as an apology.

But the strangest thing. Whoever she looked at appeared to have the features of a rabbit. Her boss had long upright fluffy ears which waggled as he spoke; her Mum twitched her nose exactly as a rabbit would and Len seemed to have developed a habit of rubbing the side of his face with the side of his hand and, when he walked ahead of her, he had a fluffy cotton ball tail. Now the question was… would this last all month?

Writing for Pleasure Book 2

Spring

Spring Season by Jean Newman

I decided to look up the season of Spring in the dictionary – no, not the internet - and at first it seemed not to be there. Well, of course, it was, but well down the list of the many meanings of the word Spring; in fact, it was marked as number nine, almost hidden amongst the many explanations that preceded it. I looked up Summer, Autumn, Winter - much more straightforward; one paragraph only for these seasons and although they could become adjectives, they remained as nouns solely as seasons of the year. Suddenly it all seemed to fit into a pattern - summer, autumn, winter, all clearly defined in writing and in reality. Summer conjures up sunshine, warmth, holidays; Autumn, straight away, falling leaves, vibrant colours; Winter, cold, snow, Christmas.

Spring, however, is different; so many things define it. As in the dictionary it stays hidden, - in the shadow of the previous winter until, suddenly, there is movement. It comes quietly, gently, almost caressing us with that special feeling that things are changing. Trees and bushes, that the day before were grey, wintry and sad, spring a surprise with a whisper of fresh green amongst the branches; we wonder how it happened - magic that will come again and again as the hidden secrets of Spring evolve.

The garden, like the trees, has waited, uncared for and sad, but again, one day we spring to attention; things need tidying up, cutting back, pruning. And in the garden the various explanations of 'spring' in the dictionary are very relevant - to move upwards, forwards; to appear or emerge; to develop or present unexpectedly - all so true when the first bulbs reveal their green fingers, not of new life, but of revival, revival of a season that rewards us and surprises us with its arrival every year.

Different Springs by Sheila Winckles

This is a word which can have several meanings, but my guess is that most people smile at the mention of the Spring season and warmer weather coming especially after a cold, damp winter. Looking forward to the beautiful spring flowers growing in all our gardens is uplifting and the prospect of warmer sunshine to follow in the summer months together with the possibility of a lazy holiday to look forward to.

Spring can also make us think of movement such as diving off a springboard into a swimming pool. And, of course, there are the spring tides or neap tides as they are called.

Spring is a time for new birth especially on the farms where farmers are busy birthing lambs, calves and chickens.

Another meaning of spring is in the movement of tools especially watches and clocks when they need rewinding.

Movement of a different kind is in the Forces when the men have to spring to attention for their Officers.

And finally, we all need the excitement of Spring Fever.

It's Spring by Maria Kinnersley

(*to the tune 'The Happy Wanderer'*)

Now is the time to clean the house

With dusters and with soap.

Each corner cleaned, all clutter binned,

No time to sit and mope.

It's Spring, it's Spring, it's Spring,
Now let the fresh air come right in.
It's Spring, it's Spring,
A time to clean and scrub.

I see the birds. They swoop and call,
They fly on high and dive.
Birds fall in love and nests are made
For young to grow and thrive.

It's Spring, it's Spring, it's Spring,
Birds fall in love and nests are made
It's Spring, it's Spring,
For young to grow and thrive.

Down in the ground the bulbs do grow,
The seeds produce their roots.
Soon daffodils will be on show
And flowers and trees their shoots.

It's Spring, it's Spring, it's Spring,
Let nature show its colouring.
It's Spring, it's Spring,
And flowers and trees their shoots.

Now you might think that we're immune,
That Spring just comes and goes.
But brides prepare to wed their men
And we all wear less clothes.

It's Spring, it's Spring, it's Spring,
Nights are no longer drawing in.
It's Spring, it's Spring,
And we all wear less clothes.

Spring by Doug Dunn

I really like springtime. Each day grows longer and warmer with leaves and plants budding all around. Animals and birds come to life, and I love to see swifts and swallows marking the end of spring and the start of summer. But why do we have springtime and what is spring like in other places in the world?

My astronomy knowledge tells me that seasons arise because the Earth is tilted from the Sun at an angle of 23.5 degrees. Without that tilt each day would be roughly the same as the next with no seasonal variation and each day and night lasting exactly twelve hours. As the Earth orbits the sun, the axial tilt results in the sun shining more and for longer in the northern hemisphere from April to October and more and for longer in the southern hemisphere from October to April.

Springtime also varies a lot in different parts of the world. I remember going on a holiday to Florida in February feeling it was more like a mild sunny English summer's day. Their springtime must be very hot! Then, a few years ago, I visited Malawi during their hot dry winter in July and August. Being south of the equator Malawi's spring starts in October and is the start of their rainy season.

I've never been to the North Pole, but I can imagine roughly what it might be like. On the 21st of March after six months of complete darkness, apart from occasionally seeing the wonderful northern lights, the sun would start to appear on the horizon. It would then remain in the sky for the next six months reaching a maximum height of 23.5 degrees on the 22nd of June. Remember that tilt? Without it, the sun would remain permanently at horizon at the North Pole. The same would happen at the South Pole on October 23rd.

So, springtime is quite different at the poles and in different parts of the world.

I really like and appreciate the spring in England with its lengthening daylight and warmer days.

Spring Cleaning by Sarah Sykes

Auntie Nellie, my mother's Auntie, always called it the S-Cleaning! She would write to us from her Lancashire home to inform us of her progress with the S-Cleaning

She had helped to bring my mother up when her sister, Sarah, died in childbirth.

I am named after this grandmother, who was known as Sissie.

Auntie Nellie came to visit us once in our tiny cottage in Adstock, near to Buckingham. I was about seven and my sister Lizzie was four. She'd made us each a doll's cradle. It was a shoe box, all beautifully lined and frilled, with the dolls dresses and the bed linen all made by hand. How we loved them!

But I digress from the subject - Spring Cleaning. This is what I should be doing now instead of Spring Dreaming.

Spring Again by Brenda Heale

"When it's spring again I'll bring again tulips from Amsterdam". The old song blared out of the radio just as Janice turned it on. She sighed. That had sort of been "their song" ever since they'd met on holiday in Holland, and how surprised they'd been to realise after much talk that they lived fairly close to each other at home. She'd thought it was a great partnership all those years they'd been together but now he'd gone off with a younger woman and she was alone. It was such a shock. She hadn't realised there was anything going on but obviously by the reaction of several of their so-called friends she'd been the only one to be surprised by what had happened.

Yesterday had left her feeling very low even though it was her birthday. Her friend Maggie had visited with a card and cakes allegedly to cheer her up, but Maggie was not the most positive of people. Far from it. She'd spent most of her visit telling Janice how sorry she was for her and to Janice's mind she'd rubbed it in a bit about how happy her own marriage was even though they both knew this was not totally true. It had been dreary weather too which didn't help, and Janice had been glad when Maggie finally decided to leave.

Today when Janice woke up although it was still chilly, the sun was shining. It had been a long winter, but it looked like Spring was on its way at last.

She looked out of the kitchen window as she washed up the breakfast dishes. Someone was coming up the path. An unexpected visitor. It was Bill from the gardening group. "How strange" she thought. "He's never come to the house before. I didn't even realise he knew where I lived."

"I hope you don't mind me coming here uninvited" Bill mumbled shyly. "I heard it was your birthday yesterday but couldn't get here then." He handed her a big bunch of tulips. "I wanted to bring you some from my garden, but they aren't out yet, so I got these in Tesco's. I think they import them from Holland."

"Tulips from Amsterdam" she said. "Do come in Bill and have a cup of tea."

She smiled to herself as she put the tea bags in the mugs. *I may be 70 now*, she thought, *but there's still life to be lived and it's time to get on with it.*

"Do you take sugar Bill?" she asked. "And have you ever been to Holland? It's a lovely place to visit in the springtime."

Stepping Out by Arnold Sharpe

Mid-February 2023

Stepping out, with a spring in his step, he looked down at his two small dogs. It was just coming light and all augured well for the coming day. If it wasn't for the two pooches beside him, he would be still tucked up in bed. If it wasn't for his two best friends, he would be missing this lovely start to another lovely day.

Dogs can be a real pain on a cold and blustery morning with the rain beating in your face. All that was made up for on a morning like this. The first day of the rest of my life he thought. Spring was in the air with birdsong and even some daffodils fluttering and dancing in the breeze. His mind often wandered when walking alone. Strange he thought the seasons weren't exactly changing but surly some of the plant life was. Didn't there used to be a more formal start to Spring? Late Winter into early Spring came the snow drops, followed by the crocuses. Then came the daffodils to be followed by tulips. Late Spring would be a feast of bluebells covering the woodland floors with primroses brightening the hedgerows. Now, you could see daffodils before snowdrops, tulips before crocuses. He shrugged, some of it must be down to genetic engineering.

He carried on with his morning saunter, for saunter was what it was. His older dog was now showing his age. The younger dog, however, didn't seem to mind, running wild occasionally trying to gee up the older dog.

He, he thought, was also getting old, so blaming his old friend was being disingenuous.

'Sorry old boy,' he muttered.

More people were now out and about, most, like himself, walking their dogs but not all. Cyclists and joggers were also taking the morning air. Spring he thought was definitely in the air.

A common trend he saw was a genuine uplift in spirits, shown by the smile on people's faces when exchanging morning greetings. He had met most of them many times, but he knew few names. He smiled, he might not know the people's names, but like the other morning walkers, he knew the dogs by their names.

'Hi Frodo, morning Algy nice to see you, Cindy.' and so it went.

There was still some time before the trees would show that Spring had truly arrived. Sometime before the undergrowth blossomed but Spring was definitely on its way.

The sun was now up but at this time of year, low in the sky. It was time to retrace his steps and pick up his morning paper, then home for breakfast and a deserved cup of coffee.

He looked down at his two buddies and yes, they too were ready for breakfast.

As he approached home a thought struck him. Perhaps a morning walk might be a good prompt for his local writing group.

Springtime in Iran by Rose White

Iran, once named Persia is one of the oldest civilisations of the world. Their calendar began 2.599 years ago.

The coming of spring is celebrated in a big way and for many days. Winters, like ours, are cold with snow in some regions. The emergence of carpets of white are snowdrops, hundreds of them. Narcissus seem to be dancing in the air giving off a lovely perfume.

Spring brings a new energy to the earth and its people. In this country astrologers will chart the exact time the sun, moon and the earth align in order for the new year to begin. The media will broadcast that this year it will begin on the 20th of March at 9.24 pm. Being forewarned spring cleaning is carried out in abundance until the Wednesday before when small bonfires are lit. Now is the time for the people to rid themselves of any negativity in their lives. They do this by jumping over the fires! Now a fresh flame of energy will renew them. In the homes tables are laid and adorned with flowers and all things designed to bring luck. There are live fish in bowls, gold coins, beans, food and sweets. The Letter S is considered lucky and objects starting with this are included. People embrace and promise to be better people in the new year.

Now celebrations can begin in earnest, and they carry on for 13 days. Lots of visiting each other with the special custom of the younger people visiting the older ones. On the

13th day picnics in the park take place and, the wealthy can enjoy them on a boat at sea.

Spring is such a longed-for time in many countries. In Iran its seen as their New Year. It will begin on the 20th of March at 9.24pm and will be recorded on their calendar as the 21.3 2023.What a wonderful passage from one year to the next.

Spring by Michael Dudley

During the earth's period of its yearly circle encompassing the months of March, April and May, the winter snows slowly melt, and the winter rains run off the ground.

Where does all this the water go? It disappears underground or runs in natural waterways to join other run-offs and form streams and rivers. This period of time we call Spring and reflects on the state of nature – from being dormant in winter to suddenly breaking open and springing up.

Underground, pressure builds up in the running water which fills the underground waterways. This water, running repeatedly for millennia, has created fissures in rock and soil such that the overflowing waterway springs up to the surface of the land.

And so, the underground water springs into Spring, and nature blossoms into Spring.

Writing for Pleasure Book 2

Your Favourite Activity/Pastime

Nature Interest by Peter Duxbury

Nature is all around me. I take time to look and be curious about what I see. Maybe that's a plant growing indoors and when it chooses to flower. Or trees in the garden outside the window, and when they choose to grow buds and become green. Or the type of clouds that blow across the sky, how they join with other clouds, or how the sun shines through them. Or what the dog is looking at around the borders of its territory. They're all interesting as they forever change, and what is the reason for the change?

I walk to the end of the road, to the nearest woodland and the fast-flowing brook. Will it be muddy, to step around the edges of the path? How many celandines have come out, and how many bright yellow petals does each have? Then there are new white flowers by the riverbank. How much has the water level grown with the extra rain, and what extra sections has it flooded? There are always new branches carried along by the flow. A fallen tree spans the river and collects extra branches. Eddies and currents of water swirling around them. Brighter green moss has grown on one side of the tree trunks.

Some things I collect. A different shaped, or coloured, leaf. A strand of fern, uncoiling out from the ground. A fir cone, or interesting shape of stone. Granite sparkling on one side, with white veins running through it. I'm careful to take only what I need and thank nature for providing it. At home I shade pastel colours on a board. Green at the bottom, through yellow in the middle, fading blue to the top. Arrange and stick the objects as if they grow around the stone, up the fern fronds, to the sky. Capture outer world to inner world.

Then I might translate to words, the feeling, the experience, the spirit of the place. The human nature that comes from more-than-human nature. Our place in the family of things. To appreciate and be interested in all that is around me. And to be grateful for.

A Hobby? by Jean Newman

I don't think I actually had a definite hobby. I had a go at all kinds of things and enjoyed them, but I suppose the answer is that I was never brilliant at any particular one, or that would have become my hobby.

I loved the skiing I did, but we didn't start until we were in our 40s, so you would never have seen me on Ski Sunday doing the Hahnenkamm downhill run.

So, what do I do now? Quite a few activities have disappeared with the onset of old age, (yes - it is old age, there's no use trying to give it another name); even the walks I did have shortened considerably and the gardening hours have become half hours, but my love of reading a good book has increased considerably; so that's what I shall name as my hobby.

Reading opens up all kinds of thoughts and desires. The tomes of Hilary Mantel have made me realise that I should know so much more about certain historical facts, but at the same time it has found me, perhaps as I am going to sleep, being in the court of Henry V111 surrounded by intrigue and gossip and trying to translate everyday occurrences of then into the life of today.

I suppose reading and letting yourself become part of the scene is a bit like being an actor, or actress; just for a while you are someone else, and you are young again, busy again, achieving again.

I find it reassuring sometimes, when things have become stressful, to return to a good book, and get lost amongst the pages and be somewhere else. I suppose it is an escapism, but it can help me relax and view things differently.

Sometimes a book can find you sensing the author must know you, because they are describing something that is almost intimate to you; it could be something sad or happy, or even a secret thought you've never talked about, but you understand exactly what they mean; you feel that you would like to meet and have a chat.

And you can become so immersed in a book, that you feel sad when you come to the end. What will be the story of the ongoing lives of the people in the book? This is when I think - perhaps I should write a book.

Writing Letters by Brenda Heale

One of my hobbies that many of you will find very old fashioned is writing letters. I've always enjoyed doing this. Even when I was a small child writing thank you letters was not a chore. When I was at school, I had a few pen friends which many children did at that time but over the years "life got in the way" and we lost touch.

Then back in 1997 a colleague at work was telling me how she had several pen pals, and she got me back into letter writing again. Since then, some of the people I started writing to have come and gone but I still write to several of them now. Over the years we have exchanged information on jobs, relationships, grandchildren and in some cases great grandchildren.

We've exchanged opinions on events in the news, gardening, global warming, health etc. etc. I've had pen pals in several different countries and many in Britain. Several of them I've met at various times when they've been on holiday in Devon. Sometimes they are quite different from how I've expected them to be. One lady who wrote quite long letters and I expected to be really chatty when I finally met her, but her answers were monosyllabic, and it made conversation very difficult. Some I've had numerous telephone calls with and others I now email.

One lady I used to write to is now house bound since her husband died so for the last few years instead of using the post we've emailed each other most days. Usually, it's just a brief few lines, a bit like writing a diary.

There have been a few odd characters over the years but now it's down to a smaller number and it's interesting to know how life is treating them. Some write every few weeks and some now just two or three times a year.

It's nice to get a real letter through the letter box though this hobby is now getting much more expensive than it was with postal charges going up yet again. I dread to think what air mail letters will cost now as they were already £1.85 for the lightest weight. Despite this I shall continue to write to my overseas pals. I've learnt a lot from them over the years about life in various countries.

Letters have always fascinated me, and I think they tell a lot about the writer. Queen Victoria certainly wouldn't have got "the mother of the year award" if judged by her caustic letters to her children and I remember sneaking a look at my older sister's love letters when I was little, and they were certainly interesting and very informative to me!

My Hobby by Peter Debnam

My hobbies have all been triggered by my life's experiences from an early age. But did I choose them as I travelled along life's highway, or was it more a case of following my early inclinations from within my DNA? I'm still unsure.

I recall my first day of school and playing with a table-top sandpit, where I felt a great need to place every item within it symmetrically: a sense of order immediately became crucial in my life.

Ill at five with pleurisy and pneumonia, my mother taught me arithmetic at my hospital bedside and numeracy became a love that accompanied my developing need for order. This manifested itself later at 10 when I discovered chess and my excitement at attending chess congresses during my school years.

My mother also taught me to read, again when I was ill at 5 and missing school. How I loved the 'Famous Five' adventures that spawned my lifelong love of reading, especially science fiction. The latter was triggered by Saturday morning visits to the local cinema (before TV you see) where I was mesmerised by the 50's space hero 'Flash Gordon'. I suppose the greatest early hobby influencer was when our first black and white TV arrived and the Olympics was on our screens – Herb Elliot, an Australian won the mile and I was hooked and have been running ever since – 'Thanks Herb'.

It is Christmas Day 1956, and I get an electric train set for passing my 11 plus. However, the engine failed and I was somewhat distraught! But my sister, 7 years my elder received her first gramophone and repeatedly played her only two 78's - Only you by the Platters and Singing the Blues by Guy Mitchell. I never looked back and have followed most musical genres ever since, being strongly influenced by Bob Dylan, Joan Baez and the 60' protest movement. Later in 1963 I was queuing for my first wage as a dockyard clerk with my transistor (aka 'Tranny') on when I heard 'What do you do to me' by Gerry & the Pacemakers and my love of the Mersey Beat was triggered, quickly followed by a lifelong love of the 'Rolling Stones when I heard 'It's all over now' on the radio when returning in a van from a family holiday.

It was not until 1990 when my love of classical arias flourished when listening to the 3 Tenors singing 'Nessun Dorma' at the World Cup that year. This love was consolidated in 2003 when driving home from the office with Radio 2 playing and I heard the angelic mezzo soprano voice of Katherine Jenkins.

Those of you who know me may wonder what happened to my Table Tennis (TT) – well, last but not least! Introduced to TT at our Church Youth club, I went on holiday to Butlins, Minehead and won Player of the Week, resulting in a free holiday at Butlins national finals, but only providing if I joined a local club. This I did; the local YMCA where great inspiration came whenever my team Captain's very attractive 18yr old girlfriend spectated – what a show off I was. Well, she was a young BBC journalist – Angela Rippon. I have been playing ever since!

Knitting Socks by Maria Kinnersley

I've tried many forms of knitting over the years with varying degrees of success. I invented albeit accidentally, waterfall cardigans before they became popular. As they were not in fashion, they just looked like bad knitting. But no aspect of knitting has gripped me so much as my latest current activity, which is making socks using double pointed needles.

Why, I've asked myself has it fascinated me so? Ever since my sister sent me a pattern, I can be seen on the sofa most nights working away.

My husband chuckled recently because I came in straight from a walk, picked up the needles and started with barely a pause. It has

I'm afraid to say become additive. Maybe I should start a group and call it Sock Knitters Anonymous.

It isn't as if it was easy to do. They recommend a 'flexible' casting on stitch – and there was me thinking there was only one which I've had to learn. There are at least fifteen. Then you have to get used to working with four needles, three of which have an equal number of stitches.

Forming the heel is the most exacting bit. You end up at a ninety-degree angle before knitting the part called of all things, the gusset.

So why am I finding it so compulsive? I think it may be for the following reasons: -

1. It's portable. You need one ball of wool and a set of double pointed needles which can easily fit into a handbag or discreetly placed on the sofa.

2. It gives relatively quick results.

3. It serves a practical purpose in that you're making something you can wear.

There are other motives like you can choose your colour and adapt the sock pattern to properly fit your feet, but the aforementioned ones are the main ones.

So, I must pop off now. I've some more socks to make.

This next one was read out under the suggestion 'something that was really important to us'. Whilst not a life's pleasure, I believe it was something that shaped the person who wrote it.

An Experience by Leighton King

Although it was the 5th of December, it was some ten degrees warmer than usual. The temperature had risen to 21 degrees Celsius.

I was eight years old and waiting for my father to get off work at 5.30pm.

Unknown to me, outside, a menacing grey-green cloud began to swirl, and a single tentacle reached down and touched the ground. In less than nine minutes, the town of Vicksburg, Mississippi would be ripped into the sky.

It had been a busy Saturday. I was supposed to be at the cinema with my friends but at the last minute had made other plans.

My father was busy talking to a customer so while I was waiting, I wandered towards the front of the store to investigate the strange wind noise that sounded like a hundred trains were passing.

I looked out of the two large plate glass windows that fronted the street.

A strange thing happened.

First there was a loud roar. The front door banged open. Then as I watched, both big glass windows first bowed out toward the street, then back inward before they exploded into a shower of glass shards.

I don't remember diving on the floor, but that's where I found myself. I was covered in bits of glass, but otherwise unharmed. The howling roar seemed to be moving away.

I scrambled to my feet and went to look where I had last seen my father. We met halfway. The lights flickered then went off leaving the store in darkness.

We felt our way back to the electrical department. Under my father's direction, I was given the task of putting batteries into torches and handing them out to anyone passing by. My effort created a sea of illuminated beams piercing the darkness. There was no looting. Everyone was co-operating with one another.

The fire department came and told us we needed to evacuate the building. It seemed there was a steel beam that had punctured the roof and was precariously holding up a good part of the second floor. The timing was good as we had just distributed the entire stock of Sears and Roebuck's battery powered torches.

My father closed up the store and we headed back to the car.

Outside was a vision of hell. We had to navigate fires and live wires sparking on the pavement, together with sporadic bursts of horizontal rain.

We passed automobile after automobile crushed by debris. Luckily, our car wasn't one of them.

Due to Vicksburg's location on a hillside and its proximity to the Mississippi river, experts always said a tornado could never happen here. Vicksburg had just experienced the "impossible tornado".

In less than nine minutes, nature had destroyed the city, its electrical services and initiated several fires. The gas main was broken and on fire.

In that brief time, the "impossible tornado" killed thirty-eight people, and damaged or destroyed 937 buildings (including

Sears & Roebuck). Some 1,300 people lost their homes. Twelve blocks of the city's main business district were destroyed. Fires burned. Two hundred and seventy people received injuries, and total damages approached twenty-five million dollars (1953).

Only later I learned the cinema where I should have been, was completely destroyed and two young girls from the audience lost their lives.

To this day, Vicksburg's "impossible tornado" is firmly etched in my childhood memory. The message of the nine minutes is clear. The "impossible tornado" can happen here.

As global warming and climate change take root, it becomes more important for us to understand and prepare.

"Our children's future is our responsibility"

Writing for Pleasure Book 2

Information

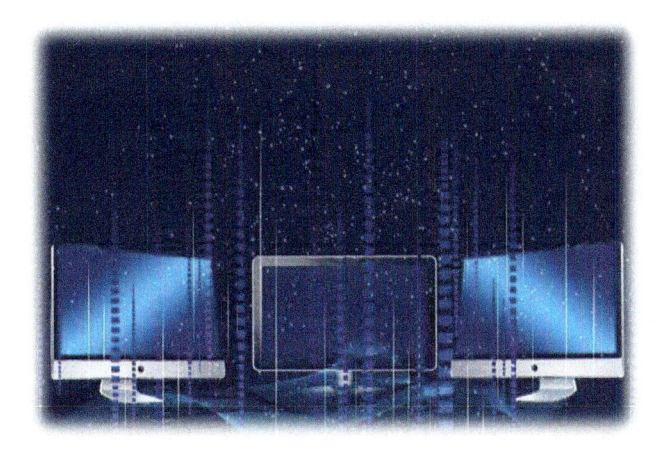

Information by Peter Duxbury

Do we live in an information overload age? Where has information mushroomed from? Did information always exist? Are we mere humans incapable of dealing with it? Or does it need artificial intelligence? Or just wisdom and enlightenment?

In 1934 T.S. Eliot wrote in the poem "Choruses": "Where is the wisdom we have lost in knowledge? Where is the knowledge we have lost in information?" This has become the hierarchy of Data, Information, Knowledge, Wisdom, ...and maybe Enlightenment. When I was at school we collected data from experiments, and we tried to interpret data to form a conclusion. Then Computing emerged for Data Processing. Computing became Information Technology and Data Processing became Knowledge Management.

By 2025 it's predicted there will be 180 zettabytes of data in the world. A zettabyte is a trillion gigabytes. Most of the data is captured then thrown away. These numbers are impressive, but still miniscule compared to the order of magnitude at which nature handles information.

However, while the natural world is mind-boggling in its size, it remains fairly constant. In contrast, the world's technological information processing capacities are growing at exponential rates. As we jump from data to information to knowledge we start to move from objective to subjective, and how much of the data is useful to humans. We decide what is of value to us based on our personal priorities, maybe in a Values Compass. If we don't know what is important to us then we can easily take in too much information, get overloaded, and manipulated for someone else's needs and priorities.

In Buddhism wisdom is defined as understanding the true nature of phenomena, from direct experience. Not from faith or scripture. If we can't see through illusion, then we should not be part of the natural world

Information by Maria Kinnersley

Her hand trembled as she gazed at the note. Her pale face worked, and she looked as if it was taking all her effort just to keep her eyes on the print.

After weeks of uncertainty, this was the news she had hoped for; had prayed for in the darkest moments of those endless nights when she lay sleepless and alone in the bed she once shared with her beloved husband, Andy.

The house seemed so empty without him and their daughter. Her eyes filled with tears at the mere thought of Alice.

There had been a row on the young girl's birthday, and she had stormed off into the garden.

Pam blamed herself for what happened next. Thinking that the ten-year-old needed time to cool off, she tidied up the tea things and took the opportunity to catch up on the news vids.

Two hours later, when she called out for Alice to come in, it had been to an empty garden.

With Andy so far away and out of contact range, it fell to her to report her daughter missing to the police. Only they'd refused to search for her.

"We have been advised by the International Space Agency," said the android in police uniform, "that that Alice Forbes is safe and well."

"Where is she?" Pam cried.

"All we know is that she is safe and well," it repeated.

She viewed her image in the hall mirror. There was no need to diet anymore, living so long on her nerves as she had been; not knowing what was happening to the two people she loved most in the world.

And now with this note, there was hope, with just one line of information.

'Pam, darling, we're coming home.'

Writing for Pleasure Book 2

Family and Friends

For Ida by Rose White

It was Easter last week and I thought of you. Remembering Easter singing, "There is a green hill far away," and you taking me and my friend Joan to church that set me on the path to finding faith. Joan and I often chatted and giggled kneeling on the hassocks. Taking us to shows at Knightstone Theatre in Weston-Super-Mare where you often seemed teary. I wondered if it was the seaside wind or the emotion of the stage show? No, years later I learned that you had an under active thyroid and realized being teary was one of the symptoms and this helped me diagnose my own thyroid condition.

Going further back leads me to wartime when one day you took me in a pushchair to an orchard where you got your hairnet caught in a tree. A friend of yours came rushing in with news causing us to race back to the house where we learned that war had been declared – I was 2 ½ years old. As the years passed, Mum and I often travelled from Bristol to stay in the comparative safety of Bleadon Village. The door was always open and the welcome loving, and reassuring. A little older and I accompanied you to Weston-Super-Mare where you helped fighting personnel to relax in the W.R.V.'s club. One of the soldiers asked you to marry him and what a wonderful wife and mother you would have made. Granny, your mother, ran a laundry with you and your sisters help so no was the answer to your suitor.

What a pity. When the laundry was ready for returning it was packed into wicker hampers and taken in Uncle Bills car to the recipients. So very white, starched and beautifully ironed it was. I remember the excitement when as an electrical iron or two were purchased to replace the old flat irons which had to be heated up on the stove. As a thank you we would go into Lyons Corner House for buns and lemonade or into Forts Ice Cream Parlor on the prom for their never to be replicated chocolate sundae. About 8 years of age I would often travel on my own, on the bus, to Weston and then take a country bus to Bleadon. No fears of being abducted in those days.

So many memories of you that I keep in my heart and so many thanks I send to you. Any creative knitting, crocheting skills were taught by you. We played games, sang songs and went for walks over the hill. You came to my first wedding and supported me when years later that union ended and later, I married again. Primrose, you said, the reason I lived so long is because I didn't get involved with men.

So Ida, how about your sister Wyn who lived only a year less than you and had quite the opposite experience?

I've had a long life full of ups and downs, compared with our calm, serene days. You lived mentally alert to 103 years of age. When you were 100 years you asked why am I still here? Ida, I said, they are not ready for such as you yet so please don't go. For all the love and happiness you gave me, I say a big thank you and wish you could see me now happy, after such a lot of sadness. But then, you probably can and one day for sure, we will all meet again.

Thank you and as you always used to tell me, count your blessings.

Relationships by Sheila Winckles

Happiness is one of the joys of humanity and for me this comes from my family and friends. There is nothing more certain in this life than that we need the companionship of our family and friends to live a happy and fulfilled life.

When God created Adam, He knew Adam needed a companion in order to be happy as well as a partner to promote the

Human Race. Now, of course the world is divided into many countries containing people of different race and colour but all with their own families and friends.

In the same way the animal kingdom is divided up into different species some wild and ferocious others domestic and friendly. All are tribal and live in their own groups and families in the same way humans too are tribal. The fortunes of families and friends depends mainly on the strata of society they are born into. Some are born into rich families or are part of the landed gentry in which case they should have less trouble being happy than a poor family who have to struggle to make ends meet as they say. This, of course, does not always happen.

The most important attribute of a family and friends is tolerance and understanding. When life is difficult, to have someone trustworthy to talk over problems which need solving is comforting especially when they are close to you.

My Family by Michael Dudley

I came from an average family and, if being brought up in the second world war situation can be classed as normal, then my upbringing was normal.

My family consisted of father, mother and three children (two girls, one boy). I recall my early years of life as being okay, but somewhat upset by my father's chronic illness.

Two things happened in my late teens though, which changed everything. Firstly, I was 'called up' to do two years national service. I left the family a boy and returned as a man. I had even learned how to shoot a gun to kill someone. I could never return to my family home as the same person again even though they tried to show me affection and love.

Secondly, my younger sister had an illegitimate child. This upset the family unit so much that these two events split us apart for many years.

Only now, after many years of dysfunction (and the death of both parents) are we three children getting together again, talking to each other, and showing love for each other.

It's never too late to be grateful.

Family and Friends by Trudy Abbott

We always say, 'Friends are the family we would choose.' However, how nice is it when your family also become your friends? I was youngest of six children and my mother would often tell me that as she separated two, another two would start fighting! She would tell us that when we grow up, we would live so far from each other, that we would be really pleased to see one another, whenever we could.

This became very true as a sister went training as a nurse; a brother joined the Air Force; another joined the Merchant Navy; and younger ones too, left home as soon as they left school. What helped to keep us united was that my mother always wrote to those who had gone, on a regular basis, and encouraged them to write home and come back to visit.

In case this sounds rather idealistic, I should say that home life was not easy, by any means. My father was an unskilled manual worker, who sometimes attained to the position of Foreman. He didn't earn a lot and gave little of what he did to my mother, to feed and clothe her and six children. Both parents smoked, and dad had a drink problem, just short of being an alcoholic. He did manage to hold down a job, but his regular boozing left us all poorer than we needed to be. It would not be difficult to dwell much on the 'hard times', but I choose to consider those worse off than me and be grateful for the good memories.

Like most of us, I lost my parents many years ago, and a brother who suffered many afflictions, too. As we age, bereavement of family members and friends will no doubt occur all too often. This is why it is so important to keep our friends and nurture all our relationships. Making new friends too, is helpful, although we will never forget those we have lost.

A Children's Story

Night Flight by Leighton King

A child's story (for 3–5-year-old)

In bed. Eyes shut tight.

Not everyone knows,

Geese can fly at night.

Overhead there were the unmistakable distant sounds.

>Honk, honk, honk

>When over the garden, the elder goose broke from the formation, floated down through the open bedroom window and landed at the foot of the bed.

>The elder goose waddled forward and asked…

>"Are you the little boy who wants to fly?"

>*"Oh yes! Can you teach me how?"*

>"Follow me," said the Elder.

>With one mighty flap, the elder goose lifted off, did a half twist and shot straight through the open window, joining the flock circling above.

>Honk

>Honk

Honk

The little boy, still in his pyjamas, rushed to the open window. He watched the geese circle the garden and gain altitude.

"Come on," honked the elder goose.

The other geese were a swirling mass of feathers lining up in their "V" formation with the elder in the lead.

Honk

Honk

Honk

"Come on, you can fly with us – just flap your arms."

As if by magic he was lifting off the floor… his voice changed to goose-speak.

Honk

Honk

Honk

He flew through the open window and out over the garden. The other geese welcomed him into the formation.

Honk

Honk

Honk

As he soared higher, the air was fresh and full of sounds.

Honk

Honk

Honk

He was full of excitement and the joy of flying.

Then there was a new sound…

RING

RING

RING

The little boy's alarm clock was saying, "Wake up!" It's time to get ready for school.

At breakfast his father asked, "Did you hear the geese last night?" The little boy smiled. Not only had he heard the geese…he flew with them!

A Creaky Floorboard Jean Newman

"Daddy, the floorboard near the window keeps creaking when I stand on it," Peter said as he was getting ready for bed. His father went to investigate. There was no creak to be heard, just shiny firm boards showing under the carpet edge.

"It does it every time I look out of the window," Peter insisted.

"Well, it's OK now and it's time you were in bed." His dad kissed him and tucked him in.

A few minutes later Peter crept out of bed and padded across to the window.

Suddenly there was a loud squeak. He knelt down and felt the edge of the floorboard; surprisingly it felt quite loose, and he managed to move it to one side. *Well, that proves it*, he thought, *I'll leave it like that to show Daddy in the morning.* Suddenly he noticed there was a little light showing from beneath the floor. He lay down on his tummy to have look and he couldn't believe his eyes when he saw a little bearded man sitting at a desk surrounded by piles of paper. He was quite at home in the large roof space above the garage. He looked up and saw Peter.

"Oh, there you are," he said, "What kept you?".

Peter didn't know what to say, "Well I told Daddy the board creaked, but it didn't when he looked."

"Of course not," the little chap replied, "It only creaks for you; it's our signal."

"Oh!" replied Peter "I didn't know about a signal, or you."

"Well now you do, so let's get down to business. I heard you talking to your mother, you seemed a bit upset about something at school. Come down so we can have a chat."

Suddenly Peter was beside the little chap and, surprisingly, they were about the same size.

"Now then tell me all about it. I'm Pedro by the way." They shook hands, and then Peter said, "I really want to be in the football team, but I'm taller than the others and a bit gangly. I trip over and fall; even pass the ball to the other side sometimes."

Pedro stroked his beard and thought for a minute or two, "Why don't you ask to have a go in goal. Being tall should help you, and your job is to keep the ball out of the net, whoever sends the ball your way."

"Oh no!" Peter exclaimed, "Jonathon Turner is the goalkeeper. He saves some amazing shots at goal."

"Right, well, it's the weekend now but we'll have another chat soon, but remember, this meeting between us is private, otherwise finding solutions becomes difficult. Off you go to bed now."

"Goodnight Pedro and thank you for listening, I'm glad I found you," said Peter happily. The next thing he was back in bed and smiling to himself as he fell asleep.

On the following Tuesday, after school, Peter ran upstairs to his room and to his relief the floorboard squeaked loudly.

He moved the floorboard, calling "Pedro, Pedro, are you there? I've got something to tell you."

And suddenly there he was beside Pedro who was smiling to himself quietly and pretending to be busy with his paperwork.

He said, "Just wait a minute, please, so many problems need seeing to."

Peter fidgeted.

Eventually Pedro said, "Now then what's all this about?"

Peter burst out, "Jonathon Turner's Dad is working in America and they're going to move over there, and I went in goal and all the team took shots and I did quite well, and I think I might be their goalie at the next match." He paused to take a breath.

"That is good news," said Pedro, "I expect Jonathon is excited. Where will they live?"

Peter stopped bouncing about, "Um, I don't know, I was so excited thinking about being in goal, I didn't ask him" and then said quietly, "I suppose I should have, instead of being pleased it meant I could join the team."

"It would have been a nice thought," said Pedro, "but you can do that before he goes at the end of term, show an interest and ask for some advice about being in goal".

"Yes, I'll do that," and then Peter said, "Pedro, will you always be here for me to chat to, and let me know when I'm going the wrong way about things".

Pedro turned and put a hand on his shoulder, "No, Peter, after this, you're on your own. You are growing up and you have to make your own decisions and to understand what's good and bad. Be proud of what you achieve, even if it doesn't go the way you want immediately. Keep trying, but it's only you that can make things work, not me. Do what you can to help others, try and make the world a happy place to be; it isn't happy for everyone, but do what you can, and it'll make you feel good."

Peter was quiet for a moment and then said sadly, "I liked knowing you were there to talk to Pedro."

"I know," Pedro replied, "But talk to your mother and father, they'll always be there for you, and ready with advice. I need to be on my way to sort out more things."

They shook hands and Pedro held Peter's hand firmly, "Good luck, Peter, remember all that I said.

"I will, I promise," replied Peter. He turned to go, but as he looked back to wave, Pedro had disappeared, and he was back in his bedroom.

A week later Peter's father said to him, "Any more creaks in the floorboard?"

"No" said Peter with a faraway look in his eye, "It doesn't creak anymore."

Childhood by Doug Dunn

When I was 11 years old, I started to make friends with a classmate David Olham who was the captain of my school year football team. One time after school we arranged to walk down to the local gravel pits with two other boys. We sat by the water looking at newts and sticklebacks and we made streams with mud and stones.

It turned out David lived right by the gravel pits, now called the Attenborough Nature Reserve. One time after school he asked me over to watch his team, Manchester United, play in the European Cup final. It was amazing to watch them on his parents' TV beat Benfica 4-1 after extra time. It was May 1968. Looking up the result has helped me think about what happened all those years ago.

What happened was I was making friends with someone I liked, and I was enjoying learning to do new things. I was learning about the family life of my classmates and how to just have fun after school.

Only now can I see that kind of fun and friendship came to an abrupt end when I moved to a new all boys grammar school. The school was about eight miles from my home and two bus rides away so there was less chance to make friends and meet after school. I was unhappy but didn't know why. I lost interest in playing football for my school and was possibly missing the friends from my previous school.

However, there was one friend, Richard, whom I got to walk with after school each day. He lived half a mile from my new school. Sometimes he invited me over to his home and we listened to singers like Cat Stevens, Mark Bolan and later on, David Bowie. After a time, he showed me how to tape his albums and play them on a cassette recorder which I had bought with my own 'paper round' money. I enjoyed making friends with Richard.

I was also bullied at my new school. Both Richard and I were often picked on at lunch times perhaps because we were friends often seen together, or possibly because he had very long hair. I enjoyed spending time with Richard and have a fond memory of going with him to see a T Rex concert in Nottingham.

Thinking and writing about my childhood is helpful. Also helpful is to think about childhood from an adult point of view rather than from how I felt as a child. It is helping me connect with people in a new fun way. How lucky to do that in such a friendly part of the world without the pressures and complications that seemed to surround my childhood.

Oslo by Arnold Sharpe

I'm Oslo the Slowworm. You may not have heard of me or more likely, never seen me. To start off with, I'm not a worm, I'm a lizard. They think I'm a worm or a snake because I don't have any legs. I'm a legless lizard. They think I'm slow, but I can be pretty quick when I need to be.

So, I'm a legless lizard. I'm grey-brown in colour. I might be a lizard, but I look like a small snake and can grow to about fifty centimetres long. You can find me in most parts of the countryside. Heathland, moorland and woodland. If you have one, you can best find me in your garden. I'm very shy and keep away from other creatures unless I'm hunting and looking for a meal. I hear or should I say feel vibrations when something moves. This gives me time to hide away usually under a rock or in the undergrowth or under garden waste that is rotting away.

Gardeners should like me because I eat slugs and snails' worms and lots of insects. My problem is, other creatures like to eat me. I have to keep my wits about me to avoid adders and grass snakes. Cats can be another problem, and I can be attacked from the air by magpies and other birds. I have one nifty way of escaping. I can shed my tail if I am caught.

Shedding my tail might sound easy but it can be difficult if not impossible to grow a new one. Any way I will do anything to fool whoever has caught me and if I'm lucky I can escape under a rock or in the grass. I must be lucky because I'm talking to you today.

I am a cold-blooded animal. This means that I spend time basking in the sunshine to heat up my body. I do this on flat rocks or paving stones.

You might think what do I do in winter when it's not as warm. Well, that's easy, I find a snug place to hide away, and I go to sleep. This is called hibernation.

So, if you want to see me don't look for me in autumn and winter. I usually wake up in spring when the weather gets warmer. As you can imagine, I am pretty hungry and spend my time hunting and eating.

If you come across me, please don't prod or poke me. Take a close look at me. I'm a handsome little fellow, even if I say so myself and I won't hurt you. I'll try to keep safe and with your help I may well succeed.

Writing for Pleasure Book 2

Games

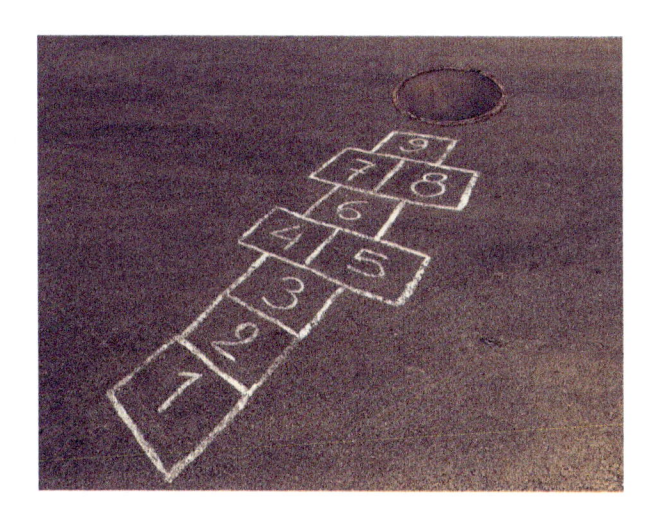

Games by Sheila Winckles

If you are like us and look back to the days when your family were young you no doubt have a cupboard somewhere with family games which are fingered and mauled. These games were produced either on holiday or at home when the children were getting fractious or bored. One would be chosen and very often it would be Happy Families.

Invariably my husband and I would look at each other and wink. How long would it be before one of the children would shout out ".I was going to put my card there.! " Out would come the sweets to bring peace and of we'd go again

Another game would be Monopoly which we all liked, and this was played in good spirits until our youngest child aged 6 would throw a wobbler and yawn and say she couldn't read the names, and couldn't we play Snap instead.

But it was the outdoor games that were the most popular like Rounders or Hopscotch. This meant taking the children to the play park where these games were available. The only drawback was we had to wait our turn which could be quite a long time so invariably we had to take a picnic or play something like

Consequences to while the time away. Then it was my husband who said he was bored and say he noticed his friend playing Bowls so he would go and join him.

In later years when the family were all old enough to keep themselves entertained, I thought now I shall do some playing for myself and I joined the local golf club with my friend. Oh! it was lovely just pleasing myself and being in the fresh air! The ladies, or girls as we liked to call ourselves, were all about the same age as myself and learning about their families brought us all closer together. In fact, some of us got together with our families and went on camping holidays which was great fun and the children who were all teenagers had a marvellous time.

Playground Games by Brenda Heale

Where have all the playground games gone? Surely someone other than me remembers the fun of paying hopscotch, oranges and lemons, what's the time Mr Wolf, Simon say and many other games. And what about leapfrog? Does anyone do that now? Not allowed by the health and safety police even if the children did want to try it.

The very little ones played 'ring a roses' or 'the farmer's in his den' in their part of the school playground, but the farmer has probably now sold all his (or her) fields for building on so I suppose he'd have nowhere to keep all the animals now.

Then there were all those skipping games with so many songs and rhymes that it's impossible to remember now. Many probably wouldn't be PC now anyway. I know there was one where you put in the names of your friends; names such as Susie and Richard sitting in a tree K.I.S.S.I.N.G. which we thought very risqué as we skipped along to it. Such innocent days.

Then there was French skipping which needed a very long piece of elastic, and cat's cradle which only required a bit of wool or string. The junior girls enjoyed all these games in their part of the playground while the rough boys played football in theirs. That was the plan anyway, although it was seldom followed. There were marbles, jacks and sometimes yo-yos which boys and girls enjoyed using if they had them.

On wet play times there were games that just needed pencils and paper. Hangman, Battleships and Noughts and Crosses.

Perhaps it's just my nostalgia for those long-ago days of grazed knees and pig tails, but it does seem a shame if these old games are gone, never to return.

Game of Life by Arnold Sharpe

First of all, what is a game? Are all games sports? Are all sports games? No, not at all. What can be said, is that all games are won or lost through taking or not taking chances. Making the correct choice can result in a win, take the wrong choice, the result can be a loss. If you take no choices or chances a positive result can only be achieved by an opponent making a bad decision. The more skilled the player, the more likely a good choice is made. This does not rule out the very important, if not the most important element. Luck. Good luck can trump the best of choices, even when playing a better player.

Therefore, it is fair to state that all games are games of chance and choice coupled with a large dollop of luck. Which makes them all the more exciting.

The biggest game of all, a game that we all must take part in, is life. Life has all the elements any good game. Choices, chances coupled with good or bad fortune. Add to this the fact that many choices, especially early in the game of life, are made for you. Only as the game progresses do those choices begin to influence the participant.

'Try,' as we must, we score 'points' on the way by achieving our 'goals'. Throughout life we all experience missed chances, dropped points and no matter how we try, we make forced and unforced errors and miss our goals.

Life is not a one-off game. It is a season of games with many fixtures. An on-form player will have the most successes. Only at the end of the season can it be decided whether it has been successful or not. Neither is it correct to say that only the player that tops the league table is the only successful player. Making the best of what you have been dealt with and hard work go a long way towards success.

What we make of our successes is important. What positives we take out of our failures can be even more important.

As a famous golfer said after a fortunate bounce helped win him The Open Golf Championship. The more I practice the luckier I get.

In the game of life, practice might not make perfect, but it sure goes a long way towards fulfilment. Which is what the game of life should be.

Writing for Pleasure Book 2

Mundane

A Mundane Day? by Jean Newman

It was time to walk the dog. The routine that she followed every morning. She walked the same way, down the lane and back across the fields. Each day was the same and had been for a long time.

However, this particular morning when she woke, Sarah felt something was different. She had a feeling she should be preparing for something, but didn't know what. On reflection she realised that it had started yesterday when instead of baking her usual Victoria sponge, she had made a stollen cake Why a stollen cake and it wasn't even Christmas.

She got ready for the walk and set off down the lane with Brandy the spaniel. She stopped when he found something interesting to check out and noticed someone walking across the field back towards the village. And suddenly, there it was again that feeling of anticipation, pleasurable even, but puzzling at the same time. Further down the lane she met her neighbour Kath who helped out Amy Walker, who ran the Guest House in the village.

"Amy's very busy this week" Kath said, "A lot of visitors; there's a chap from Germany who says he was one of the prisoners of war in the camp near here during the war. Before my time of course, but you'll remember maybe."

Back at home, drinking her after lunch cup of tea, Sarah dozed in the afternoon sunshine. Did she remember? Of course she remembered. She remembered her elderly father-in-law running the farm, while Johnny was away in the forces, and the land girls, and the POWs that came to help from the nearby camp, especially at harvest time.

What else did she remember? She remembered, the harvest lunches she prepared for the workers, the banter and the laughter, the camaraderie amongst everyone and how you could forget there was a war on, and the hard work of the POWs and their friendliness in spite of everything.

But above all she remembered the sweet smell of the hay in the barn, his blue eyes, the feeling of warmth as he held her close, and his kiss, oh yes, she remembered his kiss. But then followed the guilt, thinking of Johnny far away fighting to keep her safe, while she was being kissed by the enemy, and she remembered the desire that stayed as he walked away.

She sighed and smiled as she stirred from her reverie, just as the doorbell rang. She opened the door and there he was, his fair hair was grey, but his smiling eyes were still so blue.

"Hello Fynn" she said, "I was expecting you. I've made stollen cake."

Mundane Day? by Arnold Sharpe

Before we start, let's get one thing clear. What is mundane? It can be termed as Humdrum! Usual! Repetitious! Ordinary! Everyday! Day to Day! Wearisome! Even unexciting or uneventful.

This is odd, because I start every day walking my beloved dog and all the terms I have just referred to, can be applied to this activity. Conversely many of my walks turn out to be extraordinary, exciting, eventful and unusual.

This can only mean one thing, one person's idea of mundane is not likely to be the same as their neighbour's. Where one person enjoys Coronation Street, another may enjoy watching paint dry. To me there is little to pick between the two.

A 'Couch Potato' would not thank me for trying to show them the joys of walking.

'It's to mundane' they might say. All they would gain from a walk is sore limbs and aching muscles. Many, have no interest in a walk in the countryside. I agree, walking can be wearisome, tiresome to those who do not appreciate their environment. To many others, just to be outside in the open air is an adventure.

Standing on the brow of a hill watching the sun set can be a once in a lifetime experience. Yet, the sun sets every day. How mundane can that be?

Lots of people nowadays have so much at their fingertips, they no longer enjoy the everyday things that surround them. To them, killing alien invaders or robot warriors on a computer screen or keeping up to date on Face Book, is truer to life and more adventurous than stepping outside their own front door.

Being a grumpy old man can be very mundane, and it can take time to perfect.

There is a saying, 'if the glove fits, wear it'. I find that my glove fits as snug as a bug in a rug. I hope it's a long time before my glove wears out.

Long live mundane.

Dreamin' the Sink by Peter Duxbury

When we think of packing to go away, we sometimes say, 'Everything but the kitchen sink!' But the kitchen sink is very important, even if it's not very practical to unplumb it and try and manoeuvrer it into the car. Someone may end up with a tap on the head or drain in the back!

Anyway, back to the kitchen sink remaining in the kitchen......it is a very important place in the house. It's quite often made of stainless steel these days, and so important to keep shiny, even if that might precipitate some OCD polishing to get drip marks off every time it's used.

Sometimes it comes with a grown-up sink, and a little baby sink next to it for rinsing. But maybe the special power it has is that it is connected to three pipes. Hot, cold, and drain. I like the idea that the drain is a perfect mixture of hot and cold, yes just right! Unless you already have a fancy mixer tap, to swing arms around!

But why am I talking about kitchen sinks? You may ask! Well, it's because a seemingly mundane job can be done there. Yes, washing-up! Either dishes, pots and pans; or sometimes a bit-of-laundry. Yes, if you thought the kitchen sink is interesting enough, wait for the Washing Up!

Well, is it washing up? Or is it washing down? For those spoilsports that like to show-off with an Automatic Dish Washer – they better just leave now! Those dreadful things that waste electricity and water; and take all the fun out of it!

Yes, the fun comes in having a washing-up bowl and being able to do something useful and repetitive whilst letting your mind wander. Well, you can concentrate on getting the dishcloth around every hidden corner and crevice of cups and pans. Or you can just tie up your automatic left-brain, whilst your right-brain has creative dreams. I don't know about you, but I find the peculiar combination of being close to plumbed-in pipework and doing something repetitive is a

perfect conduit for capturing half-remembered dreams. Yes, those bizarre things you were half-way through whilst asleep....and then forgot the ending. Or worse still, forgot the dream altogether!

But somehow, I find the kitchen sink is the best place for dreams to come back. Maybe the first half, or the last half, or even some little weird bit! Yes, you can even piece all the bits together, which is even more amazing!

Until… hang on, there's nothing left in the washing-up bowl. All of its all been automatically transferred to the drainer, and all that remains is to whoosh the bowl out and wait for the gurgling noise. Unfortunately, that usually means the dreamin' stops as well. Maybe with something unusual remembered. Or start all over again with the next washing-up to look forward to. I'd do away with automatic dishwashers where you just walk away and leave them and have nothing to dream about!

Or in the words of Alan Watts in the Cunard TV advert:

'For some time, you'd forget you were dreaming.'

Mundane by Michael Dudley

Mundane is a word that doesn't exist in my vocabulary. Given that I heard and learned most of my words as a child in my family environment, that says that perhaps it was not a family word used at all. In fact, I had to look it up in Google's dictionary. It means lack of interest or excitement, dull.

I've got used to walking into town from my flat mot days. In fact, it's become a habit, such that I go through the same routine (getting ready, check the weather, check the time ((I don't want to be too early)), check shopping list, shopping bag, money, etc.), then setting off into town to repeat the same habit.

I usually feel absolutely without any interest or emotion and usually make only one decision – which café or coffee shop am I heading for?

One day though was particularly grey and the word that came into my mind was 'dull'. Oh, I thought, it's going to be a dull sort of day, and out of the blue I decided to smile at the day.

And so, I put a smile on my face and everyone I met on the way into town smiled back at me and some even responded to me with, "Hello," and continued even now to do so.

So, it seems being without interest or with a dull frame of mind may only be skin deep and can easily be overcome by wearing a lovely happy smile.

I'll leave the word 'mundane' on its page in the dictionary.

My Cardigan by Sheila Winckles

When I was young, I had a favourite aunt called Emma who was my mother's youngest sister. She and I would often go for walks together or sit and play games. Aunt Emma was also an experienced knitter and made some wonderful jumpers and cardigans for me. One in particular was my favourite. It was a cardigan knitted in green and violet wool, and I wore it constantly. Then I lost it and was inconsolable.

We were on holiday in Cornwall. The weather was beautiful, and we spent each day picnicking on the beach. I say the weather was beautiful which it was except that in the early morning having dashed there as soon as breakfast was over it was a little cool and I needed to wear my precious cardigan. Of course, later when it got warmer, I took it off and left it with our other belongings.

Later in the day when it was time to return to our holiday cottage, I couldn't find my cardigan and thought another member of the family had taken it. But they all said 'no' and I started panicking. Where was it?

Finally, my mother got a little cross with me and said we would go and call in at the police station and see if anyone had handed it in. We spoke to a very nice police sergeant who said he would keep his eyes open and look for anyone who was wearing a green and violet cardigan.

I was very disconsolate and did a lot of crying which annoyed my family. I couldn't ask my aunt to knit me another cardigan because she and her husband had gone to live in Australia.

BUT there is a happy ending to this sad story. Years later I was again in Cornwall with my friend. Jenny, and we noticed there was a Bring and Buy Sale on in the local village hall and as the weather was not good, we decided to go in and look around. We wandered around the various stalls and then I came to a lady who was selling knitwear. I gazed at what she was selling, and my eyes noticed the colours green and violet, and my heart missed a beat. I pulled it towards me just to have a look at it. Then I couldn't believe my eyes - yes It was my very own jumper. I recognised the buttons on the front which were ones my aunt had taken off a dress of hers because I had always commented on how much I liked them. I was speechless and I could feel the lady behind the counter looking at me.

"Are you alright dear.? You have gone as white as a sheet".

"Oh yes thank you. It's this cardigan. I know it's old and rather tatty looking and you will be very surprised to hear that my favourite aunt knitted it for me when I was fourteen years old. Then I lost it on the beach here in Cornwall when we came on holiday five years ago."

"How extraordinary! Well, my dear it's yours to take away. No, no there is nothing to pay."

"Please let me put something in your charity box then. I feel it's my lucky day! I must find Jenny and tell her about my adventure."

A Mundane Date by Leighton King

1963 was a teenager's summer.

Mary, Tom's girlfriend, asked if I would be willing to come along on a blind date with a school friend of hers to make up three couples for the movies. Tom would do the driving and pick everyone up.

Larry and Martha were the first couple to be collected, then me and finally my blind date, Dianne, made up the third couple. We somehow managed to squeeze Larry, Martha, me and Dianne on the back seat of Tom's '53 Ford.

Mary had warned me Dianne was shy, and she certainly had little to say the whole evening. To make matters worse the cinema had raised their ticket prices and that meant we had to pool all our money to buy tickets just to get in. There was not enough money left for popcorn or drinks.

The evening was rapidly turning into a disaster. It didn't help that the science fiction movie, the "Blob", wasn't that exciting. The on-screen highlight was when the 'goo' ate a cinema audience and spilled into the street.

Movie ended. It was now ten o'clock and dark outside.

Tom was driving us home one by one. My date Dianne was first to be dropped off. Tom stopped in front of Dianne's house and shut off the engine and headlights.

I got out of the car and like a gentleman escorted Dianne to her front door. Her father had kindly left the blaring porch light on and for good measure flicked the porch light on and off a few times which was 'Father- Daughter' Morse Code for "don't hang about on the doorstep".

I walked with her up the path to the front door - without looking I could almost feel the four expectant faces pressed against the misted-up car windows. The peer pressure was awesome.

I am certain they were all expecting me to be shunned on the doorstep. Certainly no one thought that I would get a good night kiss.

At the front door, Dianne extended her palm as if to shake hands. At this awkward moment when I didn't reciprocate the handshake, Diane said,

"Look, I don't kiss boys on the first date".

I had to think fast. "Ok then, how about the last?"

She laughed and gave me a big kiss. Adding, "Thank you for a lovely evening".

She still had a smile on her face when she opened the front door, waved goodnight to those in the car and disappeared into the house closing the door behind.

I managed to step backwards off the porch into a flowerbed then I literally skipped back to the car.

When I returned the remaining four cheered and patted me on the back.

It was a kiss to remember. Thank you, Dianne.

Autumn by Michael Dudley

I suddenly realise Autumn is approaching
Mostly, of course, the Sun
Declares that it will go to bed earlier
And get up later.

But other, more subtle signs are given
Of this change.
The trees start to release their leaves,
Just one or two at first.

Tell me, do you think they still have
Contact with their leaves
After they have released them?
Does a dandelion know where its
Seeds land after it releases them
To the wind?

Sitting under a fir tree an hour
After sunup
I realise that the tree is constantly
Shedding stuff
I feel I'm being snowed on.

Tell me, does the tree just lose
This stuff. Or does it deliberately
Let go?
Don't bother to reply, I don't really
Want to know.
For I can't do anything
With the knowledge.
Rather, I'll just sit, hear and enjoy the fact
That Nature knows it's Autumn.

Must Try Harder by Brenda Heale

Lots of jobs are very mundane,
The ones that need doing again and again.
Dusting and polishing, cleaning the loo,

All boring jobs that we need to do.

Vacuum the floor, ironing to be done,

None of it interesting, none of it fun.

Someone must like these jobs,

But it isn't me.

I'd rather go walking,

Or learn how to ski.

So I've failed in my homework Maria I'm sure,

But I'll try harder next time and write a lot more.

Writing for Pleasure Book 2

How To?

A Long Flight by Peter Debnam

I guide you to overcome all those fears and concerns and instead have a truly magical and memorable trip. Further, I offer you a guarantee that if you are not fully satisfied after reading this article, I will take your place on the plane without charging you a single penny!

Firstly, never travel to the airport on the day of travel – eliminate the stress of traffic delays and rail strikes!

As you walk to your plane, soak up the sleekness and majesty of the aircraft and note that air travel is by a long way the safest form of transport! For every 1 billion passenger miles in a car 7.2 die but for a plane it is 0.07!

So, climb aboard and feel the warm welcome from the air stewards and if you're premium economy or higher enjoy the free glass of bubbly! You reach your seat and find a cozy banket, ear plugs and a pack of toiletries. It's all looking very promising and you're already feeling better.

You have your personal video screen inviting you to select a movie from 160 of every conceivable genre. Browsing alone takes you an hour and you haven't even noticed that take-off came and went!

Before you have time to watch your chosen film you are interrupted by a steward tempting you with a 3-course meal with wine. Enjoying your meal you also admire the view below passing over the European Alps and reminisce over past holidays there. This brings on a short nap prior to enjoying your video of choice.

Then it's time for in-seat exercises or a walk around the cabin. No sooner have you returned to your seat, than coffee and snacks arrive and you while away your time viewing your screen's flight path and wonder at the distance you've already travelled. You view your second video, and the cabin lights are dimmed. Soon you find yourself in the hands of Morpheus.

You are awakened by your steward offering you a hearty breakfast which you thoroughly enjoy. This is soon followed by a cockpit announcement informing you that you will be landing shortly. So, you turn to your wife and say 'Where have all the last 17 hours gone, it seems more like a couple of hours'. She turns, smiles sardonically and says, 'Are you and I living on the same planet, dear!!!'.

Any Answers? by Arnold Sharpe

We've all watched TV news programs and listened to radio news bulletins. 'Now that's a very good question'. How many times have we heard that at the start of an answer to a question. Many times. And many times, this is the start of an answer given by a politician. The answer continues to give facts and figures not associated with the question or on many occasions, an answer that does not relate to the question being asked in the first place.

Starting an answer with, 'now that's a very good question', often means, 'give me a moment to think of a way of 'how to', not answer the question'.

Throughout our upbringing and education, we are shown or taught 'how to'. 'How to', is that a positive? One would hope so. But. In writing this exercise I am going to try hard 'how to' not write anything about 'how to' do something. My reader, will have noticed that whilst writing about 'how to' I have so far avoided solving the problem of 'how to.'

My reader may have also noticed that whilst I am trying hard to find a way of or 'how to' avoid writing about 'how to' do anything, I am finding it hard, 'how to' not get frustrated. If I am successful in writing this exercise, I will have succeeded in 'how to' not write something about 'how to' do anything.

So far, I have used the words 'how to' twelve times, sorry, make that thirteen times. Is thirteen an unlucky number? If so, I'd better use the words 'how to' once more.

I am now running over in my three-hundred-word allocation for this exercise. 'How to?' Now that's a very good question, is where we started. I have tried explaining 'how to' do nothing about anything. Unfortunately, I may have just about managed, 'how to' write three hundred words and more of gobbledegook and gibberish about something.

If this is the case, I have failed in writing 'how to' write nothing about 'how to' do anything whilst succeeding in 'how to' confuse myself.

One final observation. Would I know 'how to' make a good politician?

Staying in Charge by Brenda Heale

The most important thing about being in charge is to start as you mean to go on. When you first arrive, they will think you are the cutest thing ever, so make sure you assert your authority from the start.

Choose where you want to sit and where you want to sleep and customise the furniture involved a little to suit yourself. A few scratches here and there will make it look much nicer.

Demand plenty of attention, but when you have had enough let them know it. A little bite or scratch is usually sufficient to get your message across.

When it comes to feed times make sure they are to suit you. Ideally fresh food available both day and night on demand and be sure that you are offered the very best food. The more expensive it is the more they will value your choices. Show delight in your new food for the first few mealtimes when it's given but then suddenly refuse to eat that flavour and just stare at them when it is served up. It's always more fun to do this just after they have been shopping and stocked up on that food.

As you get older demand more freedom. Stay around the house for a few days and then disappear for many hours if not days on end. This will keep them on their toes. They will soon be putting notices on face book for your safe return at any price. It all makes them appreciate you even more. To use yet another clique "treat 'em mean to keep 'em keen". They will be so thrilled and excited when you finally stroll back through the door again.

    If you keep to these suggestions, you will have an easy life with plenty of good food and lots of time to snooze, and isn't that just what every pet cat needs?

Writing for Pleasure Book 2

Eavesdropping

Overheard by Jean Newman

Jim and his brother Rab were enjoying a meal of steak and chips, their last treat of the day. They had come to Blackpool on the annual summer work's outing, several coaches full of men and their families, from two large engineering works in Glasgow. They had all had a good time, and it was obvious that many of the men had enjoyed the Sunday opening hours of the English pub, something that was not enjoyed back in bonny Scotland.

"Och, it's been a great day", said Rab, "But we need to be off soon tae meet the buses fer the trip hame, the drivers'll no wait fer latecomers, it's a lang trip home and we need to be on time. Come on Jim".

But Jim didn't answer, he was trying to hear what was going on between the landlord and a man at the next table, who had obviously had quite a lot to drink.

"Shush, Rab, will yee nae listen to what's going on behind"

Rab listened.

"Come on old chap," said the landlord, "I think you've had enough, time you were off home, where do you live?"

"22 Henrietta Street, Glasgow", came the slurred reply, and then came tones of, "I belong tae Glasgow, dear old Glasgow toon."

"My goodness", said Jim, "He must be one of us, he'll be in nae state tae get the bus on time, we'd best take him alang wi us."

They took an arm each, and managed, with a lot of stumbling and singing, and cursing, to find their bus and explained to the driver about their extra passenger.

"There's nae time tae find which bus he came on", said Jim, "He says he lives in Henrietta Street so drop us off there when the time comes, and we'll see he gets hame"

Roughly four hours later, in the small hours of the morning, Jim and Rab found themselves outside 22 Henrietta Street, still supporting a very drowsy and muddled man, who they had managed to find out during the journey, was called Andy McFadyen.

Rab knocked on the door and waited. No reply, no movement; it was all quiet. He knocked again, and then, impatiently, started banging hard against the door with his fist.

Suddenly the window above in the house next door, flew open and a very angry face appeared, and yelled down at them, "Ye can bang as hard as ye like, but nae one'll hear ye, they're all awa in Blackpool fer the week and they'll nae be back until next Sunday," and with that the window was closed with a bang.

What happened next, I will leave to the reader's imagination.

Gift

A Gift by Maria Kinnersley

"Oh no!"

Alice's mum looked up from her slice of toast.

"What's wrong?" she asked. "I thought you were going through your birthday cards."

"It's Aunty Kath," Alice said. "I've just opened her present and it wasn't what I was expecting."

Her mum glanced across. There in Alice's hand was a small open container with thread needles and scissors.

"What a lovely gift," she exclaimed, "and so useful."

"Hm," was the response. "From the shape and size, I thought it was something else."

Her mother shot her an inquiring look. Alice dropped her head.

"I thought it was a gift card," she muttered. "I had plans if I got money for my birthday."

"Now, Alice," her mum said briskly, "you know your aunt likes to give you useful presents. And she did teach you to sew." She sniffed. "I think it's a lovely present. You should keep it in your handbag. You never know when you might need it."

"It's not going to get me a job though," said the girl sadly. "I so want to work in the clothing industry and at the moment there's nothing available."

"Well, enough of these negative thoughts. Come on, you've got other presents to open."

Six months later, Alice sat in the reception of 'Clothes by Allan.' A job at there as a receptionist had been advertised in the local paper.

"Go on, apply," said her mother. "You never know where it might lead."

To her surprise, Alice received a letter requesting her to come for an interview, which was why she was waiting here in reception.

A man entered the building. As he did, the door dropped back and caught his sleeve, ripping it.

"Blast," he said, "and just before my meeting too."

"Maybe I can help?" Alice said.

"How?" he looked doubtful.

"I can sew a bit."

He handed her his jacket. "See what you can do then," he said.

The receptionist started to speak to him, but he put a finger to his lips with a smile unnoticed by the young girl who reached into her bag and brought out a small sewing kit. Absorbed, she worked at the small tear with careful stitching.

"You seem to know what you are doing."

She flashed him a smile.

"My Aunty Kath taught me to sew."

Then, she went back to her work.

Repair complete, she handed the jacket back. He examined the repair.

"That's a good job," he said. "You can barely see the damage. Thank you."

With a wink at the receptionist, he went on his way.

The receptionist looked over at Alice.

"Mr Allan will see you now. Third door on the left through those doors, she indicated the way.

Alice knocked on the door and entered. There behind the desk was the man whose jacket she had just repaired.

"You're…" she stuttered.

"Mr Allan," he said with a smile. "I do believe you'd be wasted as a receptionist, don't you, Alice? Fancy a job at my workrooms instead?

A Short Word? by Peter Duxbury

Gift. It sounds so simple. Four letters. One vowel. Letters 7, 9, 6, 20 in the alphabet. Adding up to 42. Scrabble letter scores 2, 1, 4, 1…….adding up to 8. Not a very valuable score!

Should we really value everything by numeric scores?! The origin and meaning of Gift is really rather complex and interesting for such a short word. Coming to English from Old English and Proto-German. From invaders to this land, or when we were all joined by Doggerland. It appears in German, Norse, Swedish, Frisian, Dutch, Danish, Icelandic, Afrikaans with similar spelling, but rather different meaning. In other languages it usually means Poison, or to Marry. Or a wedding gift or dowry like a large amount of money or property, which may cause dispute or jealousy.

Maybe not spoken until someone dies. In Greek and Latin, it comes from the word "dosis" meaning an amount of medicine, or poisonous drink. Why would that be?

Perhaps we receive gifts at any time of our life, and we don't realise their meaning. Giving something is not to satisfy a want but maybe a need. Most things happen for a reason. That it takes someone else, or lifetime to discover. People and things come into our lives to learn something from. Some lessons may be pleasant. Some seemingly hard. So, a gift does not have to be a thing. It may be an ability to discover, like musical or creative ability. Maybe we don't know we have until we try, or risk ego to discover. Egos can be rather fragile. By attacking or defending instead of receiving and accepting.

So, when thinking about gift-giving at Christmas consider the acts of giving and receiving. need instead of want. And it may not be a thing at all.

And maybe we could be open to gifts at any times of our lives.

Don't look a gift-horse in the mouth!

Footnote: my own life was saved this year by the "poisons" derived from rattlesnake venom and deadly nightshade. For which I am truly grateful.

The Gift by Rose White

What on earth was she thinking about, Mary asked herself. It's in the deep mid-winter alright.

Fancy leaving the fire where they'd toasted bread with Gran's toasting fork and watched for pictures in the flames.

Just because her best friend had chivvied her, "You know it will be fun being with the gang." So here they were --- a group of teenagers leaving the town behind them, tramping along a snow-covered road. No cars, so quiet and still, who'd be stupid enough to travel out anyway, Mary thought. The cold crept into her fingers and toes, nose felt icy too.

Fun, Angela had said, was it? Well, there was chattering, singing --- boys shouting (showing off as usual). Ghostly echoes or deep silences at times. Mary began to relax and even joined in.

Up another road, they came to the quarry. Here heaps of small stones were piled twenty-five feet or more high. On summer nights this same merry band had climbed up and jumped off from the top. The winner being who had landed furthest down.

Different now, eerily quiet, blanketed in snow. Felt a bit like pioneers they did --- crunching sounds, footsteps on virgin snow. Only silent for a few seconds, then --- "Come on", then "Don't be slow", "Watch me", and off they went.

Angela had gone too --- typical Mary thought. Unsure she was, felt alone. Then, "Come on Mary, I'll help you." It was Joe that, gentle brown eyed boy --- like me he is, she thought. "Give me your hand," he said, and she did. The cold left her, she felt warm, and a sensation that something wondrous was beginning. It was.

Years later, especially on cold wintry nights, Mary thought back to that time, to the beginning of a relationship --- no, more than that, a love affair destined to last two lifetimes.

Shouldn't be sad she'd tell herself. Joe's no longer here, but my memories are. Thank goodness I went out on that night, so cold, so silent. Not so much a bleak midwinter, but instead the best Christmas present ever.

Christmas Gift by Brenda Heale

Someone's coming along the road
Whoever can it be?
I think it's that new lady
from number 23.

I've only spoken to her twice.
She really doesn't seem
much like my kind of person
with her coat of vivid green

It really doesn't go
with a skirt of blue and red
And looks a little common
As my mother would have said.

I wonder what she's carrying.
It really looks to me
like some enormous Christmas gift
to put beneath the tree.

I wonder what's inside it.
Something full of Christmas cheer.
Oh no, it really looks like
She's bringing the present here.

What can I give her in exchange?
It will really have to be
that expensive tin of biscuits
that I'd bought for Christmas tea.

I'll have to go and wrap them up
and I'd better write a card.
Losing them for a gift that I don't want
is really very hard.

Then I'll have to re gift her gift
As it won't be right for me.
I'll give it to the cleaning lady
When she makes my cup of tea.

Not that I usually give her
a gift for Christmas day
But I'll have to do it this year
Or with me it will stay

But no, the lady's turning,
Taking the Christmas gift next door.
Oh dear
Why doesn't anyone give me presents
anymore?

The Best Gift of All by Arnold Sharpe

It came out of the blue. One moment all was well, the next a feeling of puzzlement. My right arm and right leg were not responding to what my brain was telling them. An hour later after ringing 111, I was told that an ambulance was on its way.

Fast forward three days and I was laid, wide awake, at 2 o'clock in the morning, in my hospital bed. Earlier there had been some activity two beds away. The curtains now remained closed. Two nurses arrived and closed the remaining curtains on the ward. Moments later I could see the silhouette of a bed being wheeled past. I had never spoken to the man, but it was obvious that he had passed away.

Why? I will never know. The word gift came into my mind. After being given the word gift as our prompt for our December writing project, I had been struggling with the task. Now I had something to write about. I did not know the gentleman who had died but during the previous day I had seen a number of visitors arriving to see him. The only thing they had of him now, would be memories.

Memories are, by definition things that have already happened. From birth to final breath, memories are being created. Memories can soon go out of mind, but they can never be totally forgotten. Memories whether good or bad, happy or sad are legacies each of us leave scattered about during our lifetimes. In death it must be a blessing if we are remembered at all.

That being said, I do not want to sound morose. It is not my intension to be so. I intend to go on living and creating memories for a long time to come. I hope to upset those who deserve it, I hope friends and people I know enjoy my company, as much as I enjoy theirs.

Memories are archives of our lives and hopefully they outlast any material legacy we may leave behind.

Giving memories for people to remember, might, just, be, the best gift of all.

A Winter's Tale

Toronto - 1971 by Roy White

The further north I drove that morning, the effects of the storm became more obvious and the clearance of the snow less obvious. By the time I got to Sheppard the ploughing had proved less effective. And on Sheppard Avenue itself, ploughing clearly had not even occurred; at least not since some considerable time before the snow stopped. The road surface was, at best, churned up snow on top of a thick layer of ice; not conducive to maintaining a tight schedule.

"Do your best," said the Inspector looking miserably cold, through the open driver's window as the waiting passengers piled on, "The bus from the east side hasn't got here yet, so you've got a bit of a headway to carry." There was a lot of industry along Sheppard West, with a big de Havilland plane factory at Downsview, amongst many other big businesses.

I ploughed on picking up a good load, and after the intersection at Dufferin I ceased caring about the schedule and just did my best to keep going with the standing room only load, cold, mostly silent passengers getting on and off in dribs and drabs. The road was very treacherous so there was no point in rushing, and pulling up at the stops was a bit hit and miss as to where the bus eventually did stop, with the result there was some grumbling from passengers who had to walk a few extra yards in the snow to get on. I ignored the moans, and just smiled and said: "Slippery". Mostly, they accepted the explanation, it was after all glaringly obvious, but one guy who was covered head to foot in snow down one side, did have a go.

"Judging by all that snow you're carrying about your person," I said, "You're having trouble keeping your feet, why do you think it's any different for the bus?"

He just took his transfer and joined the happy throng: "Move right down the bus," I hollered, "More happy travellers waiting to join you."

My former conversational partner shuffled down the bus with the rest of them; they looked like a group of Emperor penguins, waiting for the Antarctic winter to subside … All that was needed was that David Attenborough would appear, microphone in hand to give a breathy commentary, and the scene would have been complete. Inside the bus it was cold and damp, the heating, the tracked in snow and the damp penguin look-alikes were serving to create a foggy internal atmosphere with the result that the windscreen was misting over, which the defrosters were struggling to compete with, I had to open the driver's window to have any hope of seeing where I was going; not ideal.

The ice and snow made for a difficult morning, but what was going on outside made it all worthwhile, to me anyway.

The sky was a limpid blue, dark to the west and translucently light to the east where the sun had risen in all its glory. Then, as I looked up from watching the farebox as passengers boarded, the most strikingly beautiful natural scene I have ever witnessed, before or since, appeared momentarily. The light from the sun, which was behind an enormous tree, probably an oak, struck at just the right angle and sparkled and shone on all the twigs and branches, glazed to perfection by the ice, and covered on the upper sides by a thick layer of brilliantly white snow. It took my breath away; that picture of sun and sky; tree and ice and dazzling white snow will stay with me forever. This was a truly beautiful example of God's wonderful Creation – and some say it all happened by accident.

A Winter's Tale by Brenda Heale

It was Christmas Day, and of course, it was raining. A heavy non-stop drizzle. The microwave Christmas dinner for one had been very disappointing. A couple of slices of wafer-thin turkey and very little else. Nothing like the appetising meal pictured on the box.

Susan felt low. She thought back to last Christmas spent with friends Joan, June and Margaret. Joan was now in a home, her mind totally confused by Alzheimer's. Margaret had gone to live in a granny flat at her daughter's and now spent most of her time baby sitting while her daughter went to work, and June had passed away ironically on her birthday back in June.

They'd had quite a jolly time together last Christmas. How quickly things had changed.

Susan sat by the electric fire and wondered whether to make herself yet another cup of tea. She'd dropped off to sleep during the King's speech, which was a shame as she had been looking forward to watching that. There was nothing much else on TV together other than the Call the Midwife Christmas special at 9, which she enjoyed apart from the birth scene where she looked away or shut her eyes.

Her mind wandered further back to when Albert had been alive. They'd been so happy together. There had been ups and downs of course as in any marriage, but all in all it had been happy times. It was sad that he had died so long ago now.

They'd never had any children. In their twenties, it had been good to be child-free and be able to travel the world. Not tied down with nappies and night feeds like most of their friends, but the years had gone by and still no babies had arrived.

Maybe we should have adopted a child, thought Susan, but at the time they'd always seemed enough for each other, and when Albert got ill and died suddenly in his fifties, that was that.

Anyway, children were a mixed blessing. Joan had three but not one of them ever bothered to visit her now in the home they'd found to put her in. *Too busy with their own lives I suppose.*

This really did seem like a long day. She wondered whether the rain had stopped and after a short struggle got up to find out by opening the front door.

There on the doorstep was a tabby cat; thin, bedraggled and very wet. *The poor thing,* she thought. *Perhaps it's a stray. Looks like it's hungry. I think there's a tine of tuna in the larder,* and she went off to get it. By the time she turned around with the tin, the cat was in the kitchen behind her. He tucked into the half tin of tuna she put on a saucer and waited for it to be refilled.

'I'll have to buy you some cat food tomorrow if you're still around,' Susan told the cat. 'I think the Co-op is open for a few hours on Boxing Day.'

The cat purred and Susan smiled. Life suddenly seemed a bit better.

A Winter's Tale by Arnold Sharpe

Preamble

There I was back in a hospital bed, three weeks after my first visit to a hospital bed. This time a different hospital. 2 a.m. in the morning. A déjà vu experience, I was wide awake with my mind running wild trying to put a different slant on Maria's latest prompt.

This time instead of the word gift running through my mind A Winter's Tale was keeping me awake. A story line came to mind. A nurse popped her head around the door and didn't seem worried about my insomnia. I asked and she provided me with some sheets of paper, upon which I scribbled down some notes that helped with the following story. If I'm in hospital for our next assignment I may have to leave this group because it is becoming too dangerous. Now comes the story.

A Winter's Tale

Donald was having a frustrating time. He was wandering about on the edge of a field. The first snow of winter had left a scattering all around. Christmas had almost arrived. He was muttering loudly, albeit, to himself. His greatest wish was to be a reindeer, and to help Santa Claus pull his sleigh full of children's dreams and presents.

There was, or is it, there were, two major problems. One: - He was a fieldmouse. Two: - Santa already had a full complement of reindeer. How he wished he was Prancer or Dancer, Dasher or Vixen, or any of the rest of the team.

Many miles away, near the North Pole, Santa was also having a frustrating time. Toys were being loaded on to an extra-large sleigh; toys were in high demand this year. He could see that loading was almost complete and ready for that once in a year night when thousands upon thousands of children would wake up to see their dreams come true. His frustration mixed with worry was, that Donner had put her foot down a rabbit hole and badly injured her leg.

Santa was pouring out these frustrations to his friend the Fairy God Mother, who just happened to be making a flying visit.

'As luck will have it' she told Santa, 'On my way here I stopped off and accidently overheard Donald the Fieldmouse muttering about wanting to be a reindeer at Christmas, perhaps I could make his wishes come true."

'How on earth can you do that,' said Santa.

'Tut' retorted the Fairy Godmother, 'If I can help Cinderella with her coach and horse's I can help Donald fulfil his wishes and, may I add, help you out with your problems at the same time'.

In a flash she was gone.

Using the same flash, to help in conserving energy, she appeared in front of Donald the Fieldmouse.

'Fear not' said the Fairy Godmother, for mighty dread had seized Donald's troubled mind. 'I bring you glad tidings and hope that they will give you great joy.'

'What do you want' stammered Donald, for in truth, mighty dread had more than seized his troubled mind.

The Fairy Godmother explained Santa Claus's predicament and told Donald, that if he wished she could change him into a reindeer.

'Wow' said Donald his mighty dread swiftly disappearing 'Can you really do that?'

'Surely' replied The Fairy Godmother. 'But only for Christmas Eve and early Christmas Day, so you will have to work hard and get the job done before you change back into a fieldmouse.'

'Wow' repeated Donald, his mind no longer troubled. 'How can I thank you enough'

And so it was, that Donald took Donners place pulling Santa's sleigh.

If reindeers could smile, Donald had the broadest smile of all on his face for the whole of the night. Far outshining Rudolph's shiny red nose.

Christmas Eve that year would forever be Donald the Fieldmouse's favourite Winter's Tale.

Winter Past by Jean Newman

January 1947. Snow had fallen, snow on snow, snow on snow, in the bleak mid-winter, long, so long ago. It was cold, oh! so cold. Not just outside, but inside as well. There was no fitted carpet to insulate against the solid floors of the bungalow. If your feet missed the rug beside the bed, there was only cold lino while you searched for your slippers, and there was no cosy radiator warming your clothes. You wriggled and squirmed to get dressed under the many blankets on your bed, the world of duvets and central heating was yet to come.

And then came the coal shortage and deliveries to households were curtailed and the saviour of the living room coal fire disappeared, while a restriction on the use of electricity followed, a whole family would have to search for respite from the cold around a small gas fire situated in the main bedroom.

There were, however, different ways in which to experience the cold of that winter. In his poem "Frost at Midnight", Samuel Coleridge writes, 'The frost performs its secret ministry unhelped by any wind...,' and that is what it did. When you awoke and padded across that cold floor and drew back the curtains, there was that secret ministry, wonderful patterns of ferns and leaves, crystals and etchings of the finest detail in the frost on the inside of the windows and beyond the frosted window was the snow; fresh snow each morning that showed no discretion between the ordinary little bungalow and the bigger, posher houses further down the crescent, all treated to the same amount of perfection, smooth, white and unblemished.

Then came the trek to the sledging hill, walking across the otherwise forbidden golf course, pulling your sledge through the deep untrodden snow, leaving your footprints and then the floundering and the laughter as you sink waist deep into the drifts that concealed the bunkers.

Eventually, you come to the hill with the stately Elizabethan mansion that looked over the snow-covered park and the frozen lake and you have to prove you're as brave as big brother and choose the steepest part, and, oh! the thrill of that downhill run.

In the evening everything changed, the light was different, streetlights, that were still so new to those that had only known wartime blackout, showed a different snow, marred by the day's activities and the night frost hardened the ruts in the road and there were different shadows and shapes hiding in the gardens. You could feel something different in the air; it was time for inter-road rivalry, a snowball fight. But there was a secret weapon, a pre-prepared snowball of amazing proportions, that was pushed and rolled from one strategic position to another, filled with snowballs in pre-cut compartments organised by big brother. There was so much hilarity, so much fun, so much camaraderie. There were chapped knees and chilblains, but no knives, no anger, no antagonism.

The thaw came and the snow disappeared and with the ending of WW2 such a short time before, there were hopes of better things to come, and they did come - or did they - sometimes I wonder.

A Winter's Tale, Tale by Doug Dunn

I know little about Shakespeare and have never read The Winter's Tale. So, some research was needed for this month's writing assignment.

Winter is a good time for reading, especially the period between Christmas and New Year. First, I thought to watch a performance on YouTube. I also remembered on my bookshelf there was a dusty copy of' William Shakespeare - the complete works. I felt a little ashamed to have never read the book and mistakenly believed it was passed to me from my ex-wife and English graduate from Oxford University. But then I saw written on the inside cover: 'To Mum, love from Richard (my brother) and Douglas, Happy Christmas xxx.' So, it belonged to my Mum. I remembered that my parents loved going to the theatre and saw several Shakespeare plays.

I looked at the contents page and found The Winter's Tale. In order of completion, it was one of Shakespeare's later comedies, written in 1612.

I chose to watch an American open-air performance of Winter's Tale. It was helpful to follow the script to see all the cast names and identify who was speaking. Not so easy in a theatre but fine watching on a TV screen. I still felt a bit lost following the plot, so it was time for more research. I remembered hearing from a member of our writing group how good the AI program Chat GPT is with brainstorming and writing stories. Perhaps it would give a quick summary of the plot and help explain the meaning of the play.

Here's the response I got when I asked GPT for a short summary:

"The Winter's Tale" is one of William Shakespeare's late plays, categorized as a tragicomedy. The play is divided into two distinct parts: the first half is a dark and intense tragedy, while the second half transforms into a pastoral comedy. The story revolves around King Leontes of Sicilia, who becomes consumed by baseless jealousy and accuses his wife, Queen Hermione, of infidelity. This false accusation leads to tragic consequences, including the death of their young son. However, the second half of the play takes place years later in Bohemia and introduces a lighter tone, with themes of forgiveness, redemption, and the power of time to heal wounds. The play concludes with a miraculous and joyous reunion, emphasizing the cyclical nature of life and the possibility of redemption and renewal. "The Winter's Tale" is celebrated for its exploration of themes such as jealousy, redemption, and the passage of time.

That was helpful, so I continued to ask how 'time' is explored in the play. The response this time was detailed, showing how the passage of time is explored in different ways: as a healer, a transformative force, in cyclic seasons and how time can be portrayed in resurrection and renewal.

The Chat GPT research encouraged me to continue watching the play.

Finally, I wrote my own Winter's Tale of how my relationship with Shakespeare has changed with time.

I didn't get on well with Shakespeare. At school I could not understand Macbeth or Henry V and l dropped English Literature as soon as I could, sticking to science subjects. Throughout my adult life, I occasionally went to Shakespeare plays and assumed other people understood and appreciated his work more than me. Now, in retirement, I have the time to get to know William Shakespeare again. He has come to life for me like Queen Hermione's statue in the final scene of The Winter's Tale!

With the help of Chat GPT, YouTube and my mum's Full Works of Shakespeare, I plan to research and get to know other plays and see some of them being performed at local theatres.

Writing for Pleasure Book 2

Diary Entry

October 16th, 1793 by Brenda Heale

I sit here with the other women doing my knitting. I'm making a blanket for the baby due soon. Yet another mouth to feed that we could well have done without, but I must admit I do feel affection for this little one when I feel the movements inside me and hopefully there are better times to come soon.

So far there's just been a couple of the usual executions at the guillotine, but a big event will happen very soon. At a quarter past noon today Marie Antoinette will be beheaded, so there is a bigger crowd than normal.

It must be almost time now. Yes, I think it's going to happen soon. They are bringing her out ready.

She seems to have aged a great deal since she was put under house arrest 4 years ago, but I suppose she is 37 now, so will look a lot different from the 14-year-old bride who came to us from Austria all those years ago. Her hair has been badly shorn, and she has tried to cover it with some sort of home-made bonnet. She's dressed in white as befits a French royal widow.

I missed the king's execution a few months ago as one of my children was too ill for me to leave. I hear that some of the

Queen's children have died. There was always doubt about their parentage anyway as it was 8 years until she was pregnant and rumour had that the King had problems in that department, but I know the grief of losing a child so I would not wished that on her.

The crowd is jeering as she's brought forward, but she keeps her composure and does not cry. She accidently steps onto the executioner's shoe and I hear her say, "pardon me sir. I did not do it on purpose."

She has been brought so low and looks so shabby now. I know people tell me I am too caring, but I can't help feeling a little sorry for her. They help her into position and Madam Guillotine does her job.

Even though I have seen this happen to several others, I cry out in horror this time, and, oh no! When I look down, I've dropped several stitches of my knitting. Now I'll have to unravel it all and start again.

The Decision Makers by Rose White

Of course, I wasn't in that room on September 3rd, 1939, when Great Britain decided to declare war on Germany. No ordinary people were, only those who decided the future for us. Whatever – so many lives were to be turned upside down by those decision makers.

There I was, two and a half years old, sitting in my push chair in an orchard. It was a favourite place to go, and I was my beloved Aunt Ida. The orchard's trees grew Morgan Sweet apples – the smell and taste stay with me still.

I was giggling and pointing at Ida, because she had caught her hairnet in the tree. She was laughing too as she concentrated on disentangling the fine net. Our laughter stopped abruptly when her friend hurried in and said: "War's been declared Ida, you'd better get home quick".

Ida's expression changed, no more smiles. That troubled me, I felt like crying. Not for long though because we were soon racing back to the cottage, with me hanging on for dear life to the sides of my pushchair. I didn't understand the severity of that announcement, but I was soon to find out.

With my parents back to Bristol we went. Eventually to the noise of bombs falling, waiting for the sounds of enemy aircraft and even worse, later on hearing the engines stop, holding our breath, waiting for the explosion as the V1 bombs hit a target. I saw many a bombed outbuilding site, playing on them later on.

Sadness was all around, neighbours died; our windows blew out; the slate front steps split. I carried a gas mask everywhere and learnt to hide under the stairs when a raid was on, longing for the all-clear to sound. The carefree little girl I was changed, I became hesitant and fearful.

My father and older brother joined up. Brother Bruce was wounded; we went to London to visit him in hospital. I remember sitting up in bed in the hotel eating a ham sandwich! What a luxury after all the food rationing!

Sometimes we went back to the cottage, in the village just outside Weston-Super-Mare. There was always a loving welcome and a respite from life in a wartime city.

No, I wasn't actually in the room on that fateful day. Had I been, would a little girl have made those decision makers think again? Probably not. I wasn't to know what being at war would mean, but surely with the experience of World War I they did.

And once again it wasn't to be the war to end all wars, was it?

July 7, 1880 by Jane Shann

Woe holds me tightly in its grip, for I am engulfed in deep despair and anguish. I endeavour to pen my words, falteringly so, my quill stumbling upon parchment already so intricately laced with the spray from the torrent of my tears. Edward has arrived home from Milan. I had waited with such excitement to hear about his conversations concerning the education of the deaf and dumb, the advances that would make our son's life easier and ensure his standing in society.

I had no inkling that his arrival portended such devastating news. My heart has been torn asunder into a multitude of pieces, scattered across the desolate wasteland of my soul, dead like winter leaves with no hope of rebirth. If only I had travelled to Milan, but it would have been considered unseemly for me to bother myself with the conversations of men. Perhaps I would have knocked some sense into their heads if I had. For do they not know what they have done?

The cage in which our son must now sit is racked with silence, the silence of the affliction from which he had escaped. Escape seemed such an easy ideal that Edward and I solicited with the assistance of Sarah, herself of the same affliction, yet eloquent in her assembly of self-expression to all.

Edward is adamant that Sarah will continue to instruct our son, even though she and our dearest Thomas are no longer allowed to use the language of the deaf and dumb. I have watched their fast-moving fingers and hands fly with abandon, talking, laughing together as they discuss this and that. I am slower. I stumble and stutter over hand movements that are awkward, my aging hands finding shapes a little harder now, elusive to my attempts to offer clarity.... But what reward, when my son's face and eyes light up with understanding, nodding, and continuing our discourse.

How will I converse if I too cannot wield my hands, instruments of love that God provided, to communicate with those that cannot hear? Together we are condemned to a world of silence, through the callousness of these men, who cannot know anything of feelings, or love or tenderness for another human being, regardless of whatever troubles their birthing brings. And what can we do, for neither I nor my husband have the power nor the wit to challenge this inhumane decision.

Context

Life in the United Kingdom in 1880 was marked by significant social, economic, and political changes.

For deaf people, it marked a critical point in the history of deaf education with the Second International Congress on Education of the Deaf held in Milan in 1880. At this conference, a resolution was passed favouring teaching through speech and banning the use of sign language in the education of the deaf. Consequently, deaf children were not allowed to use their hands to communicate, deaf teachers lost their jobs and sign language was banned* worldwide from the education of the deaf. Those who could not hear enough to learn to talk, were rendered to a lifetime of struggle, unable to read or write. 'Milan 1880' is infamous in the history of the worldwide deaf community, for its role in destroying the hopes and lives of those with profound deafness. (* except for one school in the USA)

1st May 1945 by Jean Newman

Yesterday evening we went into town on the bus. I'm not allowed to stay up late very often and I wondered where we were going. It wasn't quite dark as we set off on the top deck of the bus, but as we drove along, I began to notice that things were happening that I had never seen before.

The town was all alight; it was magical. Everywhere different shapes and sizes on top of the lamp posts were all shining and bright, like lanterns hanging in space, and some special ones that were sort of curved and had little pieces of glass making them look like jewels.

I made my way from seat to seat looking down all the side roads to try and see different lights and calling out to Mummy and Dad when I saw something different. One lady asked my dad why I was so excited, and he told her that I had never seen the lights before as I had only known the years of blackout.

Of course, the main road was lit up too, but not by the special shapes that you could see down the side roads, especially in the old part of town, although you could now see far ahead, and the lights gave the town buildings different shapes and shadows that looked so different than in the daytime. As we came down the hill towards the city centre, the Council House was all bright and shining in the dark and the stone lions on each side were all lit up, too. Some of the shops had stayed open later to celebrate this special time and their windows were bright and inviting. It was like looking at a different safe place that made me forget for a moment the dark places that were bombed that always make me feel so sad and a little afraid.

When we were walking home afterwards and looking for the saucepan shape in the stars like we always do, it didn't seem to be as clear as usual and the other stars we always looked for weren't as bright either. Mummy said perhaps they were a little bit sad that the new bright lights I had discovered that evening meant that I would forget to look at the stars.

I would NEVER do that.

A Battle by Arnold Sharpe

I had been pondering long and hard over which was the most significant event in British history. Sitting back in my chair, I came to the conclusion that the Battle of Hastings must come high on my list.

When was it? Ah yes, 14th of October 1066. Almost a thousand years ago.

A lovely Autumn Day on the south coast. For six thousand souls who were present that day, this would be their final autumn day.

I was there! The noise, the screaming and shouting of men resounded all around me. By the position of the sun, it was late afternoon. The battle must have been going on for many hours. Honours seemed to be even, Harold held the high ground, and his troops were repelling yet another of William's ferocious attacks.

I was wearing a chain mail jerkin, a conical leather helmet fitted snugly on my head, I carried a battle axe in my right hand a sword hung at my waist. I was away from the main battle line with a group of men, who seemed to be senior officials. Nobody asked who I was or checked anything about me, so I supposed that I must be known.

It did not take long to realise who was King Harold. He stood, not ten feet away from me and was talking earnestly to two other men who, I presumed, must be his brothers Leofwine and Gyrth.

I was suddenly struck in a quandary. If my history lessons were to be believed, I had a reasonable idea of what was about to happen. It was late in the day and the fortunes of battle were about to change. Should I offer advice on

William's tactics. And, if by doing so, Harold won the battle, I would be changing history for ever.

History told me William, who was French, won the battle and was the last successful foreign invader of Britain, hence the title Conqueror.

It occurred to me that the Normans, the Angevins, the Plantagenets, the Houses of Lancaster and York and all the following Royal Houses would never have existed……never have ruled England, if Harold won this battle.

On further thought my quandary deepened. I, me, my family and I would also…. never have existed. By giving advice, I could, in effect, be committing suicide. Then again, how can you commit suicide if you never existed?

Throughout history France has never done us any favours. In recent history General de Gaulle tried but failed. I am not a fan of France, and neither am I partial to its wine. I looked around and below I saw the Normans lining up for yet another attack. My mind was made up.

To hell with history. I would offer my advice. I stepped towards Harold. A foot shot out. Tripping, I fell forwards, headlong, hitting my head on the hard ground. Stunned, I slowly came too, I could see and hear arrows falling all around me. The noise of battle seemed to be getting nearer, louder, the screaming, the shouting of the soldiers more intense. I felt an agonising pain in my back. I had been struck by an arrow.

    I sat bolt upright, my chair rocking backwards, where on earth had I been? Suddenly, I could remember clearly…. Hastings, the sound of battle had I talked to Harold? If so, had he taken heed or had he ignored my advice? I touched myself. I suppose he must have ignored me, or, I must have been too late. A further thought occurred to me. If Harold had won the battle, I would never have existed; therefore, I could never have been at Hastings in the first place.

    Which beggars a question regarding chickens and eggs and also how and what was I doing there. I suddenly winced in pain, I rubbed my back, where had that pain come from?

History. Where would we be without it!!!!

Che Guevara - 25th November 1956 by Peter Debnam

I first met Ernesto 'Che' Guevara in 1956 in Tuxpan, Mexico through a secret source as he, alongside Fidel Raoul Castro were preparing their trip to free Cuba of the Batista dictatorship.

Briefly, Cuba was an economic disaster; four years of corruption and cronyism, with the Americans owning nearly all the sugar mills and tobacco companies and US mobs dominating gambling, prostitution and pornography, even the middle classes were disillusioned. Illiteracy was 50% in rural areas, and medical care, indoor plumbing and electricity was available only in city areas. Even the beaches were privately owned by the rich!

It was this appalling backdrop that led me to the revolutionary group as I felt that as a journalist, this was probably going to be the hottest story around in the foreseeable future. Boy was I right, but about the journey was I wrong. I now understand the full meaning of 'to hell and back'! I will begin.

On the 25th of November 1956 at 2am we waded through the waters of the Tuxpan river in Mexico. I was standing next to Che as I helped load weapons and uniforms aboard the

GRANMA, a 1943 11.5metre motor yacht. It was drizzling as I boarded by a very shaky wooden plank along with 81 others! No sooner had we cleared the Tuxpan river than we entered the Gulf of Mexico. The El Norte northern wind blew ferociously, it was still raining and the huge waves which reached the roof of the vessel rocked the yacht from side to side. Che and I huddled down as best we could but along with everyone aboard, we were violently sick and freezing cold. The journey which was meant to take 5 days took 7. I had to administer Che with medication for a number of his renowned asthma attacks, and everyone aboard was severely weakened. Worse was to come as food ran out for the last 2 days!

Suddenly, the GRANMA shuddered violently as we hit a sandbar, and I just grabbed Che to stop him going overboard! We were forced to abandon ship and between us, Raoul Castro and I were last departing supporting a severely weakened Che to wade through swampland for 2 kilometres which took us 2 hours when we were constantly being bitten by mosquitos and gnats.

We then started through the sugar cane fields with the Army hot on our tails. Bullets were flying around us and suddenly I saw blood pouring from Che's neck, but a colleague and I managed to stem the blood and literally hauled Che out of the corn field just before it went up in flames.

We struggled on until nightfall reaching the lower slopes of the Sierra Mountains, exhausted we huddled together tortured by thirst and hunger.

At sunrise, Che turned to me and said that for him this was the beginning of the rebel army. But of the 82 comrades on the Granma, only 20 of us had survived. It was, therefore, all the more remarkable that both the Castro Bothers and Che had survived the landing in Cuba to go on and celebrate the success of their revolution two years later on January 1st, 1959.

SOME THINGS IN LIFE ARE SIMPLY MEANT TO BE!

The Witness by Roy White

I was walking home. I had been to visit my mother from whom I had been estranged for a while. I was trying to get back on good terms with her because, after all, she was my mother. She had become enthralled by this roving preacher who had attracted quite a following as he went around the countryside preaching his strange ideas and, some said, even performing miracles, like changing water to wine; as if.

It was, "Jesus said this, and Jesus said that, and Jesus did this and Jesus did that", and I could not make her see that he was leading people astray and denying the Law. I had heard a rabbi at the synagogue say that Jesus had claimed the Son of Man, presumably himself, was "Lord of the Sabbath" and that he consorted with tax collectors and harlots.

I was walking along the road when I saw a large crowd of people at the foot of a hill, they were surrounding a tallish man standing there talking, there were a dozen or so fellows stood behind him, and the people closer to him had sat down to give those behind a better view.

"Happy are you poor," He said, "The Kingdom of God is yours! Happy are you who are hungry now, you will be filled! Happy are you who weep now, you will laugh!" I found myself stopping and even listening to what He said: "Happy are you when people hate you, reject you, insult you, and say that you are evil, all because of the Son of Man!" And later, "Love your enemies and do good to them, lend and expect nothing back."

He went on to say many more things, and the more He said the more I listened.

Eventually He finished his sermon, and the crowd started to drift away, many talking intently to one another, some in silence. I moved away as well, back the way I had come, to see my mother and tell her what I had seen and more importantly heard.

A few years later I was in Jerusalem with my mother for the Passover, and we were witnesses of Jesus again, only this time He was nailed to a cross, at a place known as the "skull" with a crown of thorns, naked and bleeding from the wounds of a severe scourging. His mother was standing there at the foot of the Cross with a few other women, weeping.

The soldiers who had hanged Him on the Cross were there, casting lots for his garments. And Jesus said, Father, forgive them, for they know not what they do". Despite the noise we could hear what He said. And when one of the criminals crucified alongside Him, having rebuked the other criminal for slighting Jesus, asked to be remembered when Jesus came as King, Jesus said, "I promise you that today you will be in Paradise with me."

A few days later rumours began to spread around the city that Jesus had risen from the dead, and had been seen by his disciples, and others. We wondered, my mother and me. Then we started back home to Galilee and when we got there, we heard He had been seen on the shores of the Sea, talking and eating fish with His friends.

People ask me now, has Jesus the Christ risen, I say "Oh, indeed yes!".

What would you say?

Love Letter

Dearest pillow .... by Jane Shann

Dearest pillow, my steadfast companion,

You have truly sustained me throughout my life. I loved you as a child as I love you now. Then, we had such fun; you started off by being new, white, and extremely puffed up but before too long, I had dragged you into regular and insistent pillow fights with my brother. You had no choice but to join in and be bashed about by your very own partner, his pillow, both of you seeming not to sustain injuries but surely doing so. And now, somehow, you have transcended age, for you have travelled with me, house to house, county to county, not seeming to mind the company we kept, the walls and ceilings, the bed and the linen and the other pillows that accompanied us. Together we traversed the existence of my life, we laughed and we cried; we looked up into the sky wondering where we were going yet knowing that life was an infinite journey and answers to such questions were outside our realm.

What comfort you bring me when I am weary with the world outside. I snuggle down deep into you, holding you tight, for you are my sanctuary, the protector of my soul. And even during heartbreaks of my own making, you still comfort, despite my tears, my pummelling of anger, my despair at the world, at people, at injustice and at myself. You hear my soul unbarred, the secrets of my longings, my dreams and wonderings, my plans for life and my sorrows. Never a more trusted companion could I wish for, for you keep it within, in complete confidence, silent to all but I.

On dark nights, I may toss and turn yet you are there, an everlasting presence in my disturbed slumber, when, as you hold me in the most tenderness of embraces, I finally succumb to your peaceful persuasion and sleep, where our dreams intertwine as we journey together across the universe, united in both harmony and unfading love.

Dearest pillow, none may know of our love for each other, but understand that I am truly blessed to have you as my companion in life and I thank you from the depths of my heart for all that you have given me.

In tender love. x

Smoothy by Maria Kinnersley

You have become part of a routine that makes me tingle every time the job needs to be carried out. When I prepare the scene for action, I ensure that I leave you till last. I admire your patterned bodywork as your water tank fills up at the tap before taking you to rest on the ironing board. Then, you are activated, and I wait patiently for you to reach the right temperature before we begin.

You have this amazing ability to calm me. Without a word being spoken, I know that you will do the job you have been designed to do. Together with ear buds and an Archers omnibus, we work. What more could I want?

With the pile of washing to one side and you heated, we're off. I direct and you, in obedience press whatever I chose to move you. Miraculously, creases disappear, and clothes and bedding assume their rightful shape. I don't know how you do it.

I respect your ways. If I do not treat you carefully, you can burn. Oh, I know it's not intentional, but a lesson learned.

You help me with my sewing too, aiding those pieces of material to form the contours needed to change a flat piece of cloth into a three-dimensional garment. And on a lower temperature you remove the creases from a paper pattern, allowing me to cut material to the right size. What a wonder!

I hate those who say that you waste energy and that you are not required. Can't they see that you keep me smart and tidy? I love you and the way you add that distinct touch to my clothing. I would never be without you, my golden Breville iron.

Lovingly yours,

An Ironing Fan

Love Letter for Me by Peter Duxbury

I love the way you hold me. How I fit into the palm of your hand. Your smooth curves perfectly nested into my smooth curves. How we fit perfectly together, as if designed for each other. Our weights perfectly balanced. The pull of the Earth on me met by the muscles of your hand and arm.

Your intention connected with my intention. Held first with our hearts aligned. The energy and temperature of our bodies gradually becoming the same. Our energy vibrations attuned. As if we are one.

I know you have flirted with others and tried out their curves on special occasions. A soggy experience. Their looseness did not attract you to stay with them every day. To greet you each morning as you arise from bed. I am always there waiting for you. In the exact same place, we always meet. Anticipating the pleasure of coming back to each other and caressing each other's curves again.

And now is the time. Hot water has boiled. All the ingredients lined up. Fine powder constrained in the lightest of skin. Soaked in the bath until liquid has flowed through and mingled the fluids.

Spooned to the side. You suspend me above. Anticipating the plunge into hot liquid. Grabbed and squeezed. Firm pressure from your thumb against your forefinger. Other fingers gently curled around to push our curves together. Squeeze me until all fluid has been exhausted from the lightest of skin. Just enough to avoid the skin releasing its newly saturated powder.

Oh, what a relief: you lay me down. Feeling our purpose has been served. Until I look forward to the next occasion when we need each other again. And we each gain so much pleasure from each serving one another.

(What is it? A tea bag squeezer.)

A Coffee Machine by Peter Debnam

Dear Essenza Nespresso Machine,

I felt it was time I told you just how much I love and care for you. You've been sitting on the kitchen worktop for years now, probably feeling taken for granted - Not so! Firstly, all I can offer is my sincerest apologies! And to let you know that you are actually the most important artefact I possess. Yes, artefact because to be one, it has to be of historical or cultural interest, which of course, you are. Historically because in the family context, you go back many years and culturally you are a leader in the world of coffee machines; the name 'Nespresso' is the byword and embodiment of Coffee purity, throughout the world.

You are simplicity personified when it comes to usage ensuring an exceptional cup of coffee every time, with your exclusive coffee extraction technology developed in Switzerland since 1986. It is those individual capsules that give me those mouthwatering flavours and subtle aromas. I name but a few: Roma, Ispirazione Venezia, Vienna Linizio, Firenza Arpeggio, Ispirazione Napoli and Paris Expresso. You are so clever, as my taste buds instantly feel each flavour of the city of my choice and memories of my visit there come flooding back. - how did you achieve that?

Also, please give your frother a big hug from me. I regularly amuse and entertain my guests by holding it upside down; they are enchanted when the milk stays in the frother. Rather like a whisked meringue remaining in the jug!

I do, however, have a small request which I hope you will be able to grant in view of the close connections you have to your paternal masters in Lausanne in Switzerland. My dear wife has been expecting a knock on our door for an eternity as she felt she has marketed Nespresso so successfully to her complete circle of family and friends, that a personal visit from George Clooney would not go amiss!

Peter

My Love by Arnold Sharpe

Whenever I see you, my love, I struggle to keep my hands off you. Whenever I see you, my love, I feel a yearning that knows no bounds. Your figure, your shape sends shivers down my spine. From your slender waist your body leads seductively upwards to where I struggle to contain the thrill of holding you tight.

Before I burst, I must confess to my many infidelities. My many affairs with others. The guilt I bear is insurmountable yet find it impossible to hold back my desire to experience what others have to offer. It's not your fault that you appear in so many guises, shapes and sizes. It's not your fault that you and your kind stir my mind into longings that I have to fight continuously. Yesterday when I held you, my hand shook, my mind quivered in anticipation.

The reason I write this letter is not for forgiveness, perhaps it's for understanding, understanding and forgiveness for the impulses I can't contain.

I confess, I can't keep my hands off you, I'm sorry, it's my fault that I can't be faithful to only one. You may not be the only one who can deliver what I yearn for and feed my most primeval instincts.

This letter may ease the weight from my mind if not the weight I carry elsewhere, it's not your fault my darling that you come in so many shapes and sizes. But you remain my favourite.

I cannot wait until you are in my hand again so that I can feed on the delectations and temptations you freely offer.

All my love my darling SPOON.

Arnold xxxx

My Favourite by Doug Dunn

Dear bridge table

Last year I very nearly dumped you at the Teignbridge recycling centre. But instead, inspired by visits to the Bovey Repair Cafe, I saw that I could stop your felt top falling off simply with a hammer and nails.

I have decided to buy a lovely soft green cards tablecloth. I hope you like it. I like it so much I now use you every day for office admin and as a dining table.

Recently I arranged two evenings where friends and family sat around you for dinner, bridge and a game called Quiddler. Yesterday, I hand-washed the tablecloth and gave it a careful ironing. You look great!

I am pleased I decided to keep you as you are now one of my most used household items. I even use you for watercolour painting, though with a scruffier tablecloth. In fact, you have encouraged me to get back into painting which I tend to put off, thinking I'm too busy doing more important things.

It is funny how one thing leads to another. I have played bridge all my life but only recently started bridge teaching. I know you're just an inanimate household item but strangely, I think you played a part in my decision to teach a weekly beginner's class in Teignmouth. I now enjoy teaching 12 students as part of the Teignmouth U3A network. We play in a small community hall at 3 tables with pairs of students moving around from table to table every half an hour. It's fun that everyone is getting on so well, similar to how they do at our BTAT Activities.

Thank you bridge table for staying with me. I am glad not to have thrown you out and that you are something I enjoy using every day.

Grumble

A Rant or Diatribe by Roy White

A grumble, a moan, but now it's a rant or a diatribe. I used to grumble or moan about the state of the roads, now along with most of the nation's population, once started, it's a rant or a diatribe.

We live in Coombe Close, Bovey Tracey, the road on the right after the Parish Church on the left – the road which resembles a ploughed field, where the potholes are federating and forming trenches. If the white lines painted on the road a couple of months ago are anything to go by, perhaps they are going to do something about it, but they better get a move on, or they'll have to paint the markings all over again.

There is a pothole in Ashburton Road near St John's (the road was in better shape in Canon Courtenay's day), which probably qualifies as a crater, and Bovey Straights is in Straits more Dire than Bovey. Also, there formed, a couple of weeks ago, a pothole where the tarmac surround of a manhole cover outside the entrance to the Station Road car-park deteriorated badly. This is very close to the new Town Hall.

Coombe Close has been in an awful state for years, Bovey Straights for a year or two and Ashburton Road for months, so what gets attended to first? The hole outside Station Road car park and near the new Town Hall – I wonder why?

There they were this morning, three pick-ups, a small road roller, a couple of shovels, a fork or two and six men there in glorious Hi-Viz coats and trousers. One man was actually doing something, the rest watching him or something else. It reminded me of the directive which went out from the Ministry of Public Works when the 1951 Great Exhibition grounds were being built on the south bank of the Thames, to wit: "Because of the shortage of forks and shovels due to the late war, men without said implement are instructed to lean on one another instead".

Happy driving!

An Argument by Linda Corkerton

Who tells people they are blushing,

Bill Nighy grumbles,

I know when my face is flushing!

Who tells people they are shy,
My inner self grumbles,
I know! It just makes me want to sigh.

Does it really matter?
What's the point of grumbling,
Does action need to happen - or is it worthless chatter?

Eyes glaze over, what a pain.
Fumbling and grumbling,
The laptop's playing up, again!

Going round in a circle,
Bumbling and grumbling,
IKEA instructions, my face is going purple.

Eureka moment, now I know what's meant,
Mumbling and grumbling,
Solved the problem. No more torment.

The frustration stops.

Tensions ease,

The blood pressure drops.

Not always a blight.

There is a point to grumbling,

It can bring something to light.

Grumble by Brenda Heale

They grumble about the weather, too wet/too dry

Everybody grumbles and most times we don't know why.

They grumble about the government

They grumble about the rules

They grumble about the work man

He grumbles about his tools.

The oldies grumble about the young

The youngsters about the old.

They grumble about the weather again,

now too hot/ too cold.

They grumble about the cost of living
They grumble about the rent
Once you've paid for food and heating
The moneys all been spent.
Women grumble about their husbands
And men about their wives
Why don't we all stop grumbling
And just get on with our lives?

A Grumble by Jean Newman

I would like to have a grumble
About some folks on TV.
They speak far too quickly
And are never very clear
And even with my hearing aid
I find it hard to hear.

I would like to have a grumble
That, when shopping for my tea,
It would be nice that just by chance

I'll find a leafy lettuce
Just like they have in France.
But no, they come in crunchy twos
With very little leaf,
And the leaves you find in packets
Are priced beyond belief

I'd like to have a grumble,
And ask if one knows
Why that tiny little label
That appears sewn on our clothes,
Though really very titchy
Is also very itchy.
And worries at my neck
As if there's some small speck
Of something that shouldn't be there.

I'd like to have a grumble
About bottles and other things
That have tricky openings.
'Squeeze and turn', it says,

There're arrows to show you how,
But for those who do not have the strength
They simply don't allow.

But when eating apple crumble,
I suddenly feel humble,
I think I shouldn't grumble,
So what if people mumble,
I haven't had a tumble,
Although I sometimes stumble,
And I fumble in my jumble
When I cannot find my keys.
But I'm so very happy here,
I haven't got a war to fear,
I have shoes on feet,
And food to eat,
And when out shopping
There's folk to greet
And always special friends to meet!

So, all-in-all, life's very sweet.

Let's Grumble by June Weeks

Let's face it, we can't be saintly all the time so, when we feel tetchy or out of sorts, the occasional grumble will not send us to purgatory. After all, there's plenty to grumble about - the state of the country/world, a sudden shower of rain on your almost dry washing, a broken fingernail - I could go on.

I suppose a grumble could be described as releasing pressure or letting off steam. It would seem that, alas, there are folk who are walking pressure cookers and finding fault is their way of expelling pent up feelings without completely blowing their top.

Of course, there is a lot NOT to grumble about - the first snowdrops, the sun shining after dark days, a brand-new family member.

When you think about it, 'grumble' could be described as 'rumble' with a bit of 'G force'!

Not a Grumbler? by Arnold Sharpe

I sit looking at the blank sheet which is staring right back at me. How do I start writing about a grumble, after all I never grumble. It's late afternoon and the only grumble I feel is in my stomach, that must mean it's nearly teatime.

No, I never grumble. I find grumbling pointless because grumbling is usually ignored. Making one's concerns felt is almost as bad. Complaining or finding fault are often tarred with that same brush. What's the point in grumbling?

In the past, sitting on various committees or sitting in on office meetings I have brought forward many concerns. On more than one occasion I have been given this condescending answer, 'I can see where you are coming from'. Only for that concern to be passed over. On at least one occasion I have blasted back, if you can see where I'm coming from, why, for crying out loud, can't you see where I'm heading towards. I don't see this as grumbling.

However, does this make me grumpy? I expect it does. I have been told so on numerous occasions.

As the years pass, I have tried to be consolatory, but this hasn't always been successful. For some time now I have been referred to, by some, as a grumpy old man. I do not argue over the old man observation. I strive diligently, not to let my detractors down by continuing to work hard to perfect my grumpiness.

I look about me and find it hard not to be grumpy. Many times, voicing concerns, complaining or finding fault can be, or are, thought of as abusive behaviour or even hate crimes.

Some in our new, snowflake generation, like to foster this concept. This from a generation who would like to rewrite history yet struggle to decide whether they are born male or female. Surely this isn't rewriting history, it's rewriting human biology.

I could go on, but my ranting and raving will get me nowhere apart from enhancing my grumpiness. I repeat, I do not grumble, I only make comment or observations.

I remain seated and in front of me, the sheet is no longer blank. You may think that it is blank of anything constructive, that is your prerogative.

The only grumble that remains, is the one I started with, the grumble in my stomach. Now that is something I can easily sort out.

It's teatime……….

Mr Grumble by Peter Duxbury

Maybe males and females grumble as much as each other. However, this is a story about Mr Grumble. Gerald the hedgehog to be precise.

The woodland was generally a harmonious community. Crows laughing at each other in the treetops. Owls trying to scare everyone with their eerie hooting as it got dark. Mischievous squirrels running up and down the tree trunks. Mice busily scurrying around the undergrowth. All quite happy you may say.

Until..........

There it was again. They all knew that sound. And they all knew where it was bound to be coming from. Gerald of course!

Firstly, just some quiet snuffling. But then it became the usual louder grunting. It was actually woodland language for complaining about the state of the world, how things weren't what they used to be, and how every problem started with alien invaders. The rest of the animals knew the script so well they just tried to ignore it. Certainly not to be drawn into that sort of gloom, even if Gerald kept thinking he was being amusing.

Today it was about the speed of cars driving up and down the road outside the woodland.

"There they go again, they ought to have more sense, or they might crash into each other".

Not only that, one of Gerald's relatives had a close shave when he'd been caught by headlights at night-time. Luckily, he escaped. But that started the latest complaint. The rest of the animals just put it down to the fact that Gerald was getting a bit old. His once-bright bristles were going a bit grey.

Then the rest of the animals had a bright idea. They started a club for Gerald and any other ageing animals – where they could go to a remote corner of the woodland, and each complain to each other. And leave the rest of the woodland in peace!

Mustn't Grumble by Doug Dunn

How perfect it is to be writing about grumbles this month. I almost started grumbling about having to write about this as I am far too busy with much more important things!

Or are they? I have caught myself recently, thinking that my busy things to do are more important than other people's. "Let me check my diary," I hear myself thinking, if not actually saying out loud. I could be saying I'm retired and have all this wonderful free time.

April is quite a busy month for me because I organise a social event for around 80 bridge players at a hotel in Torquay; The Devon Bridge Congress held annually at the Toorak Hotel over a long weekend.

My main job is to keep track of who is playing and that their entry fees come through mostly by online payments. With just one week to go, most people have paid and are looking forward to a nice weekend of bridge by the sea. And yet I find myself grumbling that one person hasn't paid for her team. "How can she enter and not pay?" Then there's more grumbling when she doesn't reply to my reminder email.

Writing about my grumbles has helped me see they are not very different from the grumbles I used to have as a young child. Sitting in the back of my parent's car, grumbling away about being ignored or having to go somewhere like church or shopping. I'm still making those childhood grumbles as an adult when I could be sitting up in the driving seat. I could call up the bridge lady and asking her if she might prefer to pay by cheque or cash.

Grumbling isn't so bad after all. It could be an opportunity to be in communication with people attending the bridge congress; to ask if I can help and be of service to our paying customers.

Where else can I be in the driving seat rather than a backseat complaining passenger? Arr, yes, in activities like art, tennis, walking and cycling I can be more active and encouraging to others. And there are those family and personal relationships I sometimes find myself grumbling about! But that's another story and will need another 300 words.

Or maybe not!

Writing for Pleasure Book 2

The Best Holiday

Wonderful World by Audrey Cobbold

What a wonderful world that would be! We have been lucky to have had several great holidays, including visits to Rome, Lake Como, Norway, and Grindelwald in Switzerland. The weather was kind to us on all these trips.

However, my absolute favourite holiday must have been in my home country of Ireland where we spent ten days in Connemara in June, about fifteen years ago.

The weather was so hot it melted the tar on the roads; but it wasn't an oppressive heat, as it wasn't humid. You could drive for an hour and see rivers, mountains, and lakes but very few cars, and in that same hour visit a beautiful beach that was practically deserted.

We did, however, spend our days driving slowly around stopping often to admire the wonderful scenery and when we did meet anyone, they would always stop for a chat.

Ireland has its share of problems but there in Connemara, on those sunny days, it was easy to feel everything was right with the world. But what would that mean? No wars or weapons of war, no refugees fleeing war, persecution or poverty, healthcare for all, and no child going to bed hungry, education for every child, and everyone working together to limit climate change and finally, dealing with the causes of crime.

What if there could be a special trip into space for all the world leaders, so they could look down on the planet earth - a tiny part of the universe – and witness its beauty, its fragility and in some parts its destruction.

Would it encourage them to talk about seeking peace rather than conflict? To consider it their privilege not just to hang on to power- at any cost - but to be responsible for doing all in their power to make, not just their own country but the whole earth, a better place for all mankind.

In this mythical, peaceful world, the trillions of dollars spent on war and weapons of war could be used to 'feed the World' as the song says'. What a wonderful world that would be!

The Best Holiday by Jacquie Ellis

I don't like flying, and I don't like the sun.
So what do I do if I want to have fun?

When have I ever experienc'd a time
When I really could say that it felt so sublime?

I do like the snow, and I do like the cold,
But I don't like to ski. I was never so bold.

So, when have I actually fulfilled any dreams,
And walked in a wonderland? – Never, it seems!

But wait: I recall a brief time in the past,
I was crossing a meadow in Russia, so vast

With the Volga on one side, birch trees on the other.
I suddenly felt I had met with a lover.

My legs, they just buckled. I fell to my knees,

And my forehead was stroked by a soft gentle breeze.

I felt so protected, and safe, and well-cared for
A feeling I certainly wasn't prepared for.

I lived in that moment a sensation of bliss
And imagined that Heaven was something like this.

Life Holidays by Peter Debnam

For me there is no best holiday ever, there are instead wonderful cameo moments of holidays throughout my life, which I will recount for you chronologically.

I am three years old and sitting on a three-wheeler bike on a tiny circular track in Exmouth. I can recall my first thrill at racing around as quickly as my little legs would make me go faster than the other children. I experience for the first time in my life a need to win!!

It is my seventh year, and we are at our holiday caravan adjoining Par Beach. I look upward and admire our revojet attached to the van by a nylon string. The strong wind enables it to successfully maintain its height for what seems like hours, and I am proud of my dad who got it up there in the first place.

I've reached the grand old age of ten and at our hut on Tolcarne Beach in Newquay on a hot summer day. I've been entrusted to go to the beach café with our tray of cups to collect a large metal teapot filled with tea – the way it was done in those days! I successfully manoeuvre around other tourists and deck chairs and feel very grown up!

I am now an adult and on Constantine Beach near Padstow and surfing with my wooden board. It is early evening and today the tidal sand ridges are high enabling me to push off and catch the best waves. One is right behind me and breaks from around 12 feet. I catch it and surf all the way to the beach – it was the most thrilling surf of my life and remains so to this day.

It is Saas Fee, a traffic free ski resort in Switzerland. We arrive late in the evening and none of the family want to leave the hotel. I venture out alone with my video camera and experience one of those very special moments as I venture through the village and enjoy 'the sound of silence'. It is a very beautiful village, light snow is falling and only the sound of 1 or 2 tiny electric taxis laden with some very rich looking fur- clothed tourists, whom I great with 'Guten Nacht' break the silence – it was and remains as a truly magical experience of my life.

I have now reached seventy years and visit Rome, the Eternal City. Whilst there are so many memorable amazing sights, I focus on the great Gianlorenzo Bernini, sculptor and architect of so much of the baroque Rome you see today. I recall being in St Peter's which he completed in the 17th century and seeing the enormous Baldacchino which took nine years to complete, it is simply breathtaking.

However, because of my reaction, a friend then told me that I must go to the Borghese Gallery to see Bernini's sculptures of Apollo and Daphne and the Ecstasy of St Teresa. I did so and was completely overwhelmed. Each was cut from eight-foot-high blocks of Italian marble and Bernini's intricate detail was completely beyond my comprehension. Bernini himself said at the time that he worked at night by candlelight and was so tired he found his hands were being moved by God. To this day, the visit remains the greatest thirty minutes of my entire holiday life.

The Best Holiday by Jean Newman

During the early part of 1951 my grandfather announced that in the summer holidays he would take us, as a family, to Switzerland.

I was in the second form at my new grammar school in Somerset after moving from Nottingham where I was born. It hadn't been an easy year; I was the new girl from the Midlands; I was different; first form friendships had already been made, and I had found things a little difficult.

So, this announcement from grandfather was just what I needed, something to get excited about and dream about.

In my later years I have travelled to many different places, by land, sea and air and seen amazing buildings and architecture and wonderful scenery. But absolutely nothing stays in my mind like that holiday to Switzerland. In 1951 the restrictions of the second world war were, still being felt, probably by my parents more than by my two brothers and me, but we had never travelled very far, still had rationing of some things and no-one that I knew holidayed abroad.

In Nottingham we had lived in a council bungalow, we didn't have a car, we didn't eat out and had only been on a few train trips, and most outings were arranged by the church or the Sunday School.

We caught the boat train from London for the journey across the channel, I had never travelled well in occasional car outings, but the journey across the water gave me no problem, it was different and wonderful; I felt I was crossing an ocean to a distant world, a foreign land where there was so much to discover.

We travelled through France by train, where we could hear different languages being spoken, and I'm sure my parents must have been aware of the turmoil that had taken place on the land we were travelling across not many years before.

We stopped for a meal at a station buffet, I remember we all sat each side of long tables, laid out with fancy bread and hams and cheeses, and sugary buns, and - croissants - they were a new discovery, so delicious with cherry jam, and always someone waiting to give you more coffee or tea. Even before we had reached our hotel in Spiez on the shores of Lake Thun, I thought I was in paradise.

And so, eventually, we came to our hotel. We didn't know about duvets then, but there they were in our lovely room, big, soft, white and billowy, and they enveloped you and were crisp and fresh and dreamy. And we had our own bathroom, ensuite my mother said, and I had thought that having a washbasin in the bedroom when we had a seaside holiday in England, was being posh.

A tourist ticket was available to purchase for travel all around the Bernese Oberland, and oh., how we travelled, around and on the lakes Brienz and Thun, discovered little shops and special places in Interlaken, travelled up the steep Harder Bahn funicular to Harder Kulm high above the two lakes, went by mountain railway to the Schynigge Platte, visited Grindelwald, Lauterbrunnen, and from Mürren we enjoyed the feeling of flying through the air on a chairlift to the Schilthorn, where the famous revolving restaurant is situated and we looked up at shining snow and ice on the North face of the Eiger from the resort of Kleine Scheidegg.

I can recall all those names with no hesitation, etched firmly on my thirteen-year-old mind, never to be forgotten.

One day I tried out my French when I noticed a brooch a French lady was wearing at the hotel, by saying, "Oh, Il est très jolie". "She speaks French", she exclaimed to my mother. In that one instance I was a bi-lingual, well-travelled adventurer. Such confidence in one so young!

Each evening, we dined at the hotel, we could choose different dishes and there were marvellous deserts, and fruit in the middle of the table, and always a little side salad with a lovely dressing. In the morning there they were again, the croissants and the pastries. Everything was new to me, like a wonderland, and later, even more exciting, I discovered white chocolate!

When I look back my mother must have thought, whilst we were enjoying such luxury, of the restrictions that the war had brought to us and to so many families and of the atrocities that had taken place in nearby countries. One of her favourite expressions was "Aren't we fortunate ……." and I know that above everything else, this is what she would have said about that wonderful holiday.

Scilly Islands by June Weeks

Randomly, our daughter suggested that we joined forces and we four spend a week on the Isles of Scilly. We, of course, enthusiastically agreed and, at the appropriate time, packed our bags and, at the crack of dawn, headed to Penzance.

The boys' decided breakfast was necessary (potentially ill advised) before making our way to the harbour to board the Scillonian. Knowing the reputation of this crossing I prudently swallowed a dose of 'Quells' but, miraculously the sea was calm, and we arrived at Hugh Town, St. Mary's intact.

With an hour or two to explore in glorious sunshine, we then boarded the small boat for St Martins where we were staying in a quaint and cosy B&B.

Keen to get our bearings, we deposited our bags and began our exploration of the island. We walked through lanes bordered with fields of flowers, the warm air full of scent and the buzzing of happy insects, until we reached the beach and looked out over clear turquoise water towards the islands we planned to visit.

That evening, with a choice of one hotel/pub/fish and chips outlet, we opted for the latter then, as became routine, back to our digs for scrabble, books and bed.

Over the next blue skies days, we enjoyed boat trips, the tropical gardens of Tresco and delightful St. Agnes. On the one very wet and windy day, undeterred, we decided to walk to the Daymark, perched precariously overlooking treacherous waters.

The strength of the wind increased considerably to the point at which it seemed sensible to anchor ourselves together as being blown into the void was a distinct possibility. We decided that a fortifying drink was needed to calm the nerves, so we squelched our way to the hotel where we dripped in a warm corner, drink in hand.

Our return journey was a totally different scenario, and I have never seen so many green faced folk by the time we docked back in Penzance. The islands are spectacularly beautiful, and this would seem like a regular holiday but, for me, it was a very special and happy time particularly as it turned out to be the last holiday with my husband before his final illness. So, it really was my best holiday ever with a lasting legacy of fantastic memories.

With Precious Rose by Roy White

On September 2nd last year, Rose and I got married in a Service at the parish church St Peter, Paul and Thomas. It was a glorious day.

A few days later we departed for our honeymoon on the Isles of Scilly; a place where Rose had previously lived for a long time, but which I had never visited before. We went by train to Penzance; Rose's son-in-law Andy and her daughter Liza, drove us to Land's End airport and there we boarded a rather elderly plane to fly to St Mary's.

A short, but memorable flight; it was a beautiful late summer day, and the view of the islands in the blue sea was truly unbelievably beautiful.

Rose left her walking stick in the departure lounge, but they knew Rose and liked her, and the stick came over on a subsequent flight and was delivered to our B&B by one of the airport-bus drivers.

There succeeded ten days, in mostly glorious weather, of walking round St Mary's with visits to other islands as well. Most of the time Rose was striding along, with me struggling to keep up and requiring a rest at most of the available benches. Such energy she had, and always meeting people who knew her, and obviously were very fond of her.

A wonderful holiday in a glorious location with a beautiful lady, I thank the Good Lord for it and for the very special memories.

Best Holiday Ever by Doug Dunn

"Is this really your best holiday ever?" Hannah called out from across the other side of the swimming pool.

"I think so. No, definitely!" I swam over to her, about to ask if she thought the same.

"What makes it the best, though? I find it quite hard to compare holidays," she said.

"I remember people from my table tennis group saying the same as you. Holidays are so different and difficult to compare. What I like about this tennis holiday is it was just an idea that came out of the blue."

"Yeh, then everyone seemed so keen to go along with it. Angie, are you glad you came here?" Hannah called out again.

It was hard to believe just a year ago Angie completely broke her arm in an electric bike accident. She was unable to play tennis or swim for months, both activities she loved and missed terribly. But now, thankfully, she was back in action. Something like that can happen to any of us at any time.

"Actually, it was Sue's idea to come here to Spain," I said, "and deciding on

September gave us the whole summer to plan our trip."

"Shall we take a bus to the beach after playing tomorrow morning rather than stay at Jan's pool?" asked Hannah during dinner.

Jan was a former member of our Ashburton Tennis Club and good friend of Sue who just happened to own a tennis court and swimming pool in Spain!

It was wonderful to see people who I play tennis with, week-in week-out, in a completely different context. Still playing tennis but also having fun in lots of other ways. What I loved about this holiday was that we were all familiar with each other and yet there was plenty to discover.

"Perfect!" I said, "shall we all go?" Everyone seemed happy with swimming at

the beach. After all, it was too hot to play tennis in the daytime anyway.

I looked forward to the next morning, doing a bit of exploring of the surrounding area and perhaps even spotting some new birds by the coast. We were lucky to have Pete with us who worked for the RSPB, often giving bird tours in exotic places.

I remembered thinking about asking a tennis club member to go on holiday. I kept putting it off and it seemed like it was never going to happen. But I had heard of tennis clubs going on group holidays and decided that was a much better idea. And that's where the idea came from.

Perhaps this really is going to be my best holiday ever!

My Best Holiday? by Arnold Sharpe

My best holiday ever? Sorry. I don't have one! Unless, it has still to be enjoyed. Many holidays stand out but to pick one out, would be to do a disservice to the many others that have left lasting memories.

Over a period of many years, starting in the 1990s, we visited Madeira on numerous occasions, sometimes two or three times in a year. So, perhaps, it might be appropriate to mention a few incidents coming from those visits.

On our very first visit, fate took a hand. We met a young Madeiran called Amandio Rodrigue. Soon we knew his family, his friends and enjoyed many riotous parties with them.

We ate, we drank, sometimes a little too much, in many remote places not all on the tourist map.

That aside. My favourite place to visit on the island is Curral das Freiras, otherwise known as The Nuns Valley. During the 16th Century French pirates took a fancy to the island of Madeira. Raping and pillaging became their speciality. A convent of nuns took exception to this, especially the raping part, so they sought refuge. They travelled some ten miles inland and settled in a remote valley. This became known as Curral das Freiras or the Nuns Valley.

The valley lies at 2000ft. and is surrounded by mountains, the highest of which is Pico Ruivo, standing at 6000ft. The valley is an extinct volcano. Until 1953 there was no road into the valley, the only access being paths and mule tracks. The nuns truly valued their chastity.

The best way to visit this remote beauty spot is by local bus, the No.81. Ask to get off at Eiro do Serrado, a famous viewing point. You will know when you are getting near by how often the locals are crossing themselves. When you visit for a second time you also will be tempted to cross yourself. The drops off the side of this narrow road take your breath away.

There is an hotel at Eiro do Serrado but first visit the viewing platform. This will give you good reason to calm your nerves, so stop and take a drink before descending into the valley.

This must be one of my favourite short walks. A mere mile and a half but with a descent of a 1000ft. The path zigzags down the mountain side. Stop and admire the views, they are spectacular. The intrepid explorer is rewarded by a choice of watering holes before catching a return bus to Funchal.

I might not have a favourite holiday, but I do have many favourite experiences.

The Best Holiday? by Peter Duxbury

I'm not going to select the best holiday! There is no such thing as "Being Retired"! For me, all holidays are special and are a return to simplicity and connection to the cycles of Nature. If they are just a commercialised break from work drudgery it makes me ask why we ever submitted to that?

Yes, a 'package holiday' is so easy when we are too busy at work to think about truly celebrating a holiday. We're all supposed to enjoy ourselves by spending loads of money, adding to climate change by flying, over-eating fully inclusive, drinking to be happy, and impossibly not having disagreements about anything. It all becomes a bit much, to out-compete with who had the best holiday!

So, it now seems more natural to me to celebrate the eight pagan festivals aligned to our own authentic place on the Earth.

We have just had the holiday festival of Beltane around May Day to celebrate the blossoming of Nature into full life. With the May Queen and the Green Man coming together with the wild energy of Pan for love and passion.

For me that has meant camping in the bluebell woods high above the shores of Lake Windermere, celebrating the community of singing and storytelling around the fire circle. And on Dartmoor the Morris sides (teams) were welcoming sunrise at 5am on the slopes of Haytor. Something altogether more authentic than a package holiday on a crowded aircraft to a crowded beach.

Perhaps instead of 'Being Retired' we can celebrate life throughout our entire lives and turn our work into something more meaningful. Perhaps we can pass on such wisdom as Wise Elders.

To quote William C Bryant:

'Go forth under the open skies and listen to Nature's teachings...'

Writing for Pleasure Book 2

Closed Door

The Closed Door by Jane Shann

People hurried past without a second glance at the closed door. It was of a nondescript brown colour of no particular age or style, fronting an equally unremarkable small house, nestled between a quaint florist and a 'greasy spoon' café that served traditional British breakfasts and strong tea.

It had a dirty brass plaque shaped like a lion's head, and a matching handle to turn and open. Above, in ancient script, were the letters INES, itself an indication of the significance of the door, along with a long-handled pull bell to alert those within.

Unusual you might think, but no one took any notice of this or the door. It just stood there, silently observing the bustling world and the myriad thoughts that endlessly occupied the minds of those passing.

Occasionally someone would pause, intrigued by the inscription but most were too busy to look. One evening, approaching the longest day of the year, a young man came and settled on its threshold. Tired and slightly dishevelled, he sat on his newspaper, pulled up his coat around his ears for warmth and settled down to rest.

The door watched and listened. He listened to the man's thoughts; he watched the way he slowly fell into sleep and saw the beginnings of his tortuous dreams. He looked into the darkness of his mind, closing in and pulling him down into an ever-ending abyss, tossing him around, twisting him into contusion and into dark oblivion. Yet, he began to sense a potential of a silent mist arising slowly from the depths of these thoughts, upwards, lifting into the stars, into stillness. Freedom.

Reaching out, the door offered a hand. The young man uttered a long slow sigh, gave a small smile and he quietly left.

The Closed Door by Jean Newman

The demolition team were hard at work; they were making their way down the road of empty houses, exposing the fireplaces, the bedroom wallpaper, an Ascot heater on a bathroom wall, a dangling lampshade, a drooping net curtain - an encyclopaedia of people's lives laid bare for the world to see.

Down at the far end, near to the disused warehouses and the old wharves, one house, number 69, defiantly displayed geraniums in a window box, a shining door knocker and curtains at the window.

Bert Walker, supervisor for the demolition team, knocked at the door. There was no answer, but he knew that Elsie Roberts was in there. Sometimes she shouted through the window, rich words of objection to her home being taken from her, saying they could destroy the house around her.

After more knocking, Bert sighed and walked away; there were two days now before the team reached Elsie's house, then drastic action would be needed, and he didn't relish the thought. The situation was known to the Company as 'Procedure for A Closed Door', but the workers knew it as 'chaos when the buggers won't budge'.

Later that day Elsie's granddaughter, Sophie made a visit, negotiating the rubble and entering by the back door.

"Mum's sent me round to talk to you Gran", she said with a hesitant smile.

"So, what difference will that make to the situation", Elsie retorted, "I'm not moving, and the door stays closed. All my memories are here in this house, the victory celebrations after the war, your Grandad coming home safe from

Africa, the parties; your mum was born here, and the boys. There's a world of memories in this house".

"Gran, Sophie said, "It's you that holds all these memories, not the house. When it's demolished it won't tell me anything, but when I visit you, even now you've always another tale to tell me, along with everything else since I was tiny. They won't demolish the memories; they'll stay with you. And," Sophie continued, "The new flats are lovely, I've been to see them. There's a view of the river, no stairs to climb, a walk-in shower, just everything you need, all waiting for you to enjoy, another set of memories for later."

"But it won't be a memory, will it?", Elsie answered, "You'll know all about it, if it happens, and it won't, so don't think you can change my mind".

Sophie smiled to herself, "Oh, there's something else I should tell you. I wanted Rob to come with me, but he's working, I'm expecting, Gran, you're going to be a great-grandmother! Your move to the new flat will be a memory, even if not told by you, Mum and I will have so many things to tell this little person in the future. Just think how lovely it will be for you to look out of the window and show the baby all the boats on the river. You're not that old, you'll be able to tell it all about this house and bring it to life for someone who never knew it, as we do."

For some time, Elsie sat quietly, thinking, then she got up and hugged her granddaughter and said, "That's wonderful news and now you're here we should get started on the packing."

The Closed Door by June Weeks

A good fifty years ago, my mother mentioned that she had been invited to tea at an old country manor located a few miles from her village. I was invited too if I would transport her there.

On the appointed day, we drove down country lanes, finally arriving at a pair of imposing gates. We were welcomed in and led to the drawing room where we sat in deep armchairs to enjoy tea and cake.

Our hostess then asked if we would like to take a tour of the house which we enthusiastically agreed to. The rooms exuded an air of faded grandeur, and I was acutely aware of age and history.

We appeared to reach the end of our tour in the old-fashioned kitchen when I noticed a door in the corner which led to a flagstoned passage with doors to either side and a set of room bells on the wall. This was, of course, the servants' quarters, no longer in use but once a hive of activity.

As we wandered along the passageway, I noticed most of the doors were ajar and we could peep into these small rooms - lodgings to the number of maids, groom and housekeeper employed to ensure the smooth running of the residence.

On our return to the kitchen, I asked why one door which we were now passing again was firmly shut. Asking if this was a storeroom our hostess paused then opened the door indicating that I could enter.

As I stood in that small room I was completely overwhelmed by a feeling of utter despair and grief. I hastily stepped out and our hostess could see I was thoroughly shaken and said she knew how I felt as she had experienced it and had never met anyone similarly affected until now.

It appears the last occupant had been a maid, hopelessly in love which could never be fulfilled so tragically took her own life.

I hasten to add that I'm not given to flights of fancy, but I have never forgotten that bleak feeling in the room with the closed door.

The Closed Door by Peter Duxbury

It was quite a solid door. Heavy wood, opaque, apart from a security spyhole. Painted white, with a gold handle, and two gold keyholes. Was it an exit or an entrance? An exit from all that is familiar, or an entrance to a place unknown?

The boy spent his childhood happily playing in a familiar house. It had a blue front door with fluted glass window to which new visitors always came. A white rear door with fluted glass window to which neighbours and tradesmen always came. The doors were seen every day, and what was on either side of each was usually known. It felt safe.

Nothing was known of a white, opaque door with gold handles and golden keyholes.

The boy became a man, left the safe home, worked, created a new home, started a family, children went out through new doors... until all that was left was a shell. One day the man decided he would walk clean out of the door of the shell and not return. The door opened easily, and amazingly on the path outside he found a golden key. There was a key-tag that read "Key One of Two". He kept it until one day he reached a white opaque door with two golden keyholes. He tried his key, but the door did not open. He looked through the spyhole and saw a marvellous world he had never seen before.

At the same time a woman was walking on a different path elsewhere in the world and found a golden key with a tag that read "Key Two of Two". She too eventually came to a white opaque door with golden keyholes. She turned her key in the lock, and the door opened. Through it stepped a man, and the pair of them embarked on a new adventure in a marvellous new world that neither had experienced before. Both an exit and an entrance!

The Closed Door by Trudy Abbott

Have you ever faced a closed door?

One that brought disappointment to the fore?

A door you would have liked to gone through

But circumstances prevented you.

Perhaps it was the family you never had
Or the job you wanted so, so bad.
Maybe it was lack of health
That caused you not to gather wealth.

The relationship that could have been,
Or friends, when needed, were unseen.
Travel that eluded you?
You never got to Timbuktu?

If you could that door pass through
Would happiness have resulted too?
Perhaps the hope was just a dream
Or fantasies that might have been.

Not all doors are closed, all the time,
Think of those that opened fine.
Did you make the most of them?
If there's still time, reach for that gem.

The Closed Door by Sheila Winckles

Janet and Betty had been friends since they were old enough to play together in each other's gardens. Now at eight years old they always walked together to school. It wasn't a long walk but a pleasant one through countrified roads with pretty gardens.

There was one house which always intrigued them and where an old man who lived there sat in the window and waved to the girls as they walked past. The girls waved back and whilst waving looked at a dark green painted door in the side hedge.

This door intrigued the girls who would make up stories about a fairy or a hobgoblin who lived there. The door was never open, and they made the same remark that perhaps the old man would come out and explain what it was for.

Then one day their wish came true. As they were walking past the old man's house ready to wave to him there he was sitting in a chair in the garden.

"Hello girls. Off to school, are you?"

"Yes!" they said together. Then Janet said, "We have always wondered what that green door was doing in your hedge."

"It's very old and goes back to when I was young during the war. It was our air-raid shelter. We would hide in it when the warning siren went off to tell us the Germans were coming."

"Can you still go in it?" said Betty.

"No not now it has disintegrated. There is only the door left, and I keep it for memory's sake."

"Oh! We thought someone lived there", said Janet. Then she asked, "Are you able to walk?"

"No," said the old man whose name was Adam. "I now have a lady to mind me, and she pushes me into the garden when it is fine. It is grand to see you girls each morning. Work hard at school. Goodbye."

Closed Doors by Doug Dunn

Recently, I decided to open the white fence door at the bottom of my garden. For no reason except to be able to chat with a passing neighbour who might happen to drive to their parking bay. I enjoy reading in my garden with a coffee or some lunch at a small garden table.

So far, I've not met anyone, but at least I've spent more time outside than I usually do, enjoying the fresh air and birdsong from nearby cedar trees.

I also had time to wonder: Where else in my life do I have metaphorical closed doors? One I thought of was to do with bridge. Me not being willing to play with 'low standard' players. My regular Monday bridge partner is a 'good standard' but unfortunately, she has recently moved away from Bovey Tracey.

Maybe I could be willing to play with anyone of any standard who asks me for a game. I could treat it as part of my bridge teaching which I enjoy each week. In fact, one or two of my beginners said they would like to play at Bovey on a Monday afternoon when I suggested it. How wonderful that would be to see how they progress each week.

Another area where I close doors is anything to do with spending money! Now having retired and become mortgage-free I've never been better off. And yet, I cautiously put off going on holidays, buying new clothes or buying nice things for my house just in case. In case of what?

That reminds me, last month's writing assignment was about my favourite holiday. I wrote about planning a tennis club holiday in

Spain or Majorca. I now feel open and willing to make that holiday actually happen!

A Child's Thoughts by Brenda Heale

If I open that door

is it treasures galore

or monsters that snarl I shall see?

Will they bite off my head

or growl at me instead

or just ask me what I want for tea?

If it's treasures and treats

and chocolatey sweets,

I'll be glad that I opened the door,

but if it's bad things inside

then I'll wish I could hide

and keep it shut up for ever more

Is there a monkey through there

that sits on a chair

and eats biscuits he dunks in his tea.

Shall I look through the door

or imagine some more?

Mum says I watch too much T.V.

The Closed Door by Linda Corkerton

She knew she shouldn't be there. Not again. But still she loitered on the pavement below the For Sale sign – a sentry standing defiantly as if to say, 'No entry unless you can buy me'. The last of the morning's dew glistened on the surface of the board and slid slowly down onto the spongy moss below, four months in the making.

She stared at the closed front door. The months and effort it had taken her to get that door. Landlord permission, dry weather forecasts, sanding wood and sanded fingertips. The joy of the final coat of paint. Her very own front door, poster red, no-one else had a door like it in the street. 'You're find us on the right at the end of the street, the door's a pillar box red' she'd say to anyone who needed to find her. And they always did.

She remained immobile and made her decision. Slipping silently along the side path, hand over the gate, her fingers finding the bolt without hesitation from years of habit, and gently pushed.

The grass was uncut, but the flower beds were just as she had left them. Bulbs were starting to poke through, shrubs unfurling delicate leaves and bud tips waiting for warmer days. She wondered if anyone would be there to see the garden wake up or if it would keep its own company with the bees and the butterflies. Rings of grey lined the edge of the patio, ghosts of summers past, where pots of lavender, mint and heather no longer stood. The pots sat in limbo at her brother's house unconcerned. Whilst she, where was she, waiting for a new front door to call her own.

She peered in through the dusty sheen of the window at the stillness inside. The kitchen surfaces now impersonal, her imprint gone for ever. She turned away and knew in her heart this was the last time she would come.

It was the landlord's right to sell, it was his house, she had instructed herself repeatedly, nevertheless her other self still whispered but it was my home for 10 short years with only one long month to depart.

She ran her fingers over the glossy surface of the front door for the last time, the pin marks from the eviction notice the only blemish on the closed door. She could and would have a poster red front door somewhere else. And walked away.

Writing for Pleasure Book 2

Something That Scares You

A Fearful Moment by Jean Newman

We were driving back home after visiting both sets of parents in Somerset. It had been a good weekend and had given us a well-earned break following all the hard work of moving house only a few weeks before. The children were chattering and discussing the weekend in the back of the car when I heard Lisa say, "Fancy Nan having a dream about our house being burgled."

"What was that all about," I asked my husband, "Oh, you know Mum," he answered, "always interpreting her dreams into something, even when she can't remember everything that happened."

I leant back in the seat, trying to recapture the anticipation of returning to the new house and all the plans we had discussed for renovation and re-organisation; so many ideas for the extra room it gave us and how we would enjoy the large garden. But I couldn't relax and as we drove nearer to home, I felt a heavy cloud of uneasiness envelop me. As we drove into our drive the sun went behind a cloud and there was a chill in the wind as we got out of the car. I went up to the front door and fitted the key in the lock, but suddenly felt so uneasy and took a step back. The children were clamouring to get inside and couldn't understand my hesitation.

"Tell Daddy to come and unlock the door, I don't seem to be able to."

He unlocked the door and there was a rush of air and a noise at the back of the house somewhere that sounded like a door banging. It didn't sound right. I still didn't go in and let the others go before me.

"You had better come and look at this, "David said, and guided me inside. The French windows had been forced open. It was chaos everywhere, drawers pulled out, cupboards open, everything left strewn about. Because of the age of the house the bedroom doors upstairs were lockable, and I had locked them, a last-minute decision before we went away. A big mistake: each one had been forced open, rough splintered wood as a reminder of what had taken place. The irony was, there was nothing to take; we had no jewels, no priceless heirlooms; computers and mobile phones and all the other modern paraphernalia were yet to come.

For all their nasty work they were rewarded with one gold sovereign but left behind a constant awareness of any noise in the night when David was away on business, and our young daughter's reluctance to sleep in her room until the damaged door was put right and even then, would sometimes shout out and say she heard a noise.

I have never again felt anything like that awful dread I had of opening our front door that evening, so long ago now.

My Solo Flight by Leighton King

It was a perfect day for getting airborne. The sun was out at the grass airfield, and it was buzzing with activity.

I had been given a present of a "Glider Taster Experience Voucher."

When I arrived at the Weston-on-the-Green airfield, I surrendered my voucher, and my details were captured on an index card.

Everyone was invited to help out, recovering gliders, pushing them out to the launch point, connecting the winch cable and launching into the wind.

Occasionally the man with the index cards would call out a name and someone would be launched into the sky. Once the glider reached the necessary altitude, the launch cable would be released and would come down aided by a small parachute. The club tractor would retrieve the cable.

Somewhere on the side line, the man with the index cards called out, 'King…Leighton King…,' and he was gesturing that I should head toward an old orange glider with an open canopy. This was not going to be a slick high-performance glider like the one Steve McQueen flew in the opening shots of the movie "The Thomas Crowne Affair".

The old orange glider had been recovered and was already at the launch position with the canopy open. The bloke holding the wing level with his free hand was gesturing I should get in and fasten my safety harness. I thought the seat cushion came out of a lawn chair. I reflected perhaps it was designed to accommodate a parachute.

A second new person arrived and took over the job of holding the wing. I looked at the empty seat beside me and thought that maybe this person would be the instructor. Another person came and gave the tow cable a couple of shakes to see that it was secure, and I was given a thumbs up and a double pat on top of the canopy.

So, where is my flight instructor?

Something serious is happening here. I have never BEEN in a glider, and I think I am about to fly one.

A voice outside, 'Clear above and behind – UP SLACK!'

Sheeeeeit! Aaaaaaaaaaa! The glider rumbled forward.

I held the joystick, wings level. I was feeling every bump on the grass runway. This didn't last long as the old orange bird left to ground and headed skyward.

What am I to do? I am sure my heart stopped several times. A voice in my head kept saying, **'FLY THE DAMN AIRPLANE!'**

The launch cable was still attached and was starting to strain as the glider tow reached its maximum length.

'You must release the cable Leighton! Release the cable Leighton…'

There was a problem How do I release the cable? BAM! That problem was solved. The cable had just slid backward off the hook and freed itself. The glider nosed over and now the orange crate was in a dive like a Stuka bomber. I eased her out of the dive and got the glider flying straight and level.

NEW PROBLEM. I'm flying away from the airfield.

I kept repeating to myself, 'Don't get distracted – FLY THE DAMN PLANE!'

[I get increased heartrate just thinking about the situation].

Using the joystick and rudder I managed without an engine to do a gentle 180 degree turn without stalling or spinning the aircraft.

I am now heading back toward the grass airfield with the wind behind me. I swooped down to as low as I dared and discovered a main wheel brake that could be applied with the rudder pedals once the glider touched the ground.

It was surreal watching the line of parked cars go by. I held my breath. After a bumpy landing, I managed to stop before joining the ditch and the cars on the A4 with a gentle ground loop. The glider tipped to one side, and I scrambled out. I looked up and was amazed at seeing a wall of people heading down the runway towards me.

The lead person was in the air more than on the ground. He turned out to be "Commander Lord Pickled-Walnut, Chief Flight Instructor at the glider club.

His angry words, 'Were you trying to kill yourself!!!'

He was not amused when I repeated the pilot's creed: -

'Any Landing you can walk away from is a good landing.'

*****

Post Flight Debriefing

The tractor recovered the glider. There was no damage.

I explained I studying to get a PPL (Private Pilots Licence) at CAE Oxford Aviation Academy, and although at the time I only had 16 hours flying time, this was the first time I have ever been in a glider. I was told my little bit of powered flying experience probably saved my life.

The information on the index card "Pilot Experience" didn't take into account my powered flight time at CAE Oxford.

There was confusion at the handover between two launch volunteers and the winch operator. One went off to find an instructor to accompany me on the flight. The second volunteer managed to launch the glider.

That Scares Me by Jane Shann

Nine-year-old Jane swam out beyond the breakers and floated on her back, relaxing in the sunshine and enjoying the peace and solitude of the sea. She felt free and fearless, for once without a care in the world.

Turning to look at her family and see where her brother was, she waved to let them know she was alright. Her father waved back and began recording on his cinecamera, his hobby to capture these moments of the family.

But as her father watched through his camera lens, a giant and dreadful wave began building up, looming, dark and furious in its energetic compass. With horror he watched it approach his daughter, its increasing roar drowning out all other sounds, but she didn't notice.

In its fury, the wave raised its powerful head and crashed down, savagely pushing her down and tossing her round and round, smashing her against the seabed as hard as he could. Quickly she shut her eyes tight and stretched out her hands to steady herself and catch anything, rocks, stones that would stop her tumbling and slow her descent into the sea.

Above, the wave and her psyche battled, racing to be declared the winner by the gods of the sea, whilst her body was dragged further and further out into the depths, with nothing left but a breath circulating around and around.

Last year, I returned and made my peace with Copacabana at the New Year. Asking for forgiveness and understanding, I stood at the edge of the waves, my toes gently yet firmly placed in the current, in honour of the power and raw enormity of the sea. I felt my fear and distress slowly and gradually leave my body and, after some time, I turned and rejoined my brother on the shore.

Fear by Roy White

There is a great deal to fear in these benighted times, so I have struggled to find something comfortable to write about, especially as I prefer to at least try to amuse.

Therefore, I will refrain from compiling a list, you could all do that for yourselves, but instead touch on a couple of the things that have been said about fear.

No passion so effectually robs the mind of all its powers of acting and reasoning as fear.

This may be true, to a greater or lesser extent, but surely it depends on the individual; the person who becomes a quivering jelly is ill-equipped to survive, but the person who is stimulated to think on his or her feet in dangerous situations will have a much better chance of survival and become a leader. This was, of course, more true in primitive times, but still applies now. Anyway, how primitive are scenes on the streets of this country at this time?

If the above saying is true, where does that leave the "fight or flight" response? Sometimes stated as the "fight or flight or freeze" response. The above is only the freeze part, so I submit the human race would have died out very quickly.

Fear is an absolute requirement for a species to survive and always has been. My daughter's dog is a happy, constantly tail-wagging creature, but constantly on the alert for any possible hint of danger, such as post persons, or it may be men (or women) in shorts. He growls and sounds fierce, but is in actuality, totally harmless, his fight or flight response is to lick their hands, if offered.

The only thing we have to fear is fear itself.

This phrase was famously used by Franklin Delano Roosevelt in his inauguration speech of 1933, and I would respectfully submit is as equally untrue. We as species and all other species, require fear to protect us from danger. In the wild, small birds need to be constantly fearful to protect themselves from predators.

The early bird catches the worm, but the alert one lives to eat it. And this still applies to us, in this supposed modern age, we need to be on the alert to protect ourselves from those who seek do us harm as individuals or as a society, from scammers and other criminals; from other societies hostile to ours and from hostile governments, and our own politicians.

To sum up, it would be wonderful if we had nothing to fear, but that is not the case and until we are returned to Paradise, we will remain in peril, so stay alert, stay alert.

What Do I Fear? By Brenda Heale

I love all animals, insects and reptiles. I kept snakes for about thirty years and my son had all sorts of lizards, snakes and giant creepy crawlies, including a tarantula over the years that I've been happy to hold. But there's something about birds, especially in large numbers flapping around me that freaks me out.

Don't get me wrong. I would never hurt them and can happily watch them on a bird table through a window, and having been brought up in the country can name many different types. It's just having them close up and flying around that frightens me

I do like bats. They don't seem to flap like birds, even though they fly.

I blame it on the fact that I watched the horror film 'The Birds' on TV at a very young age and now I think they are just waiting to peck my eyes out! But it probably goes much further back than that as on the farm I grew up on much of our income was from chickens and their eggs, so we kept several hundreds of these birds.

Way before I was old enough to start school, I was sent out to collect the eggs. This was often no problem, but some of the chickens would decide to sit on their eggs hopefully to hatch them. As I slid my little hand under them to steal the eggs, they would stare at me with their beady little eyes and give me a nasty peck which resulted in a sore and bleeding hand. So, I have no love of chickens.

I've been a vegetarian for about forty years, but if any carnivores are coming to my house for a meal, it's always chicken I will cook for them. So, if you come to my place for dinner and you eat meat, it's roast chicken or chicken curry for you.

Seagulls also add to my phobia as I was slapped across the face by the wings of one as it stole my just bought ice cream. Other bad experiences I've had with seagulls involved one that was injured knocking me as it almost landed on my head, and another time long ago one deciding to drop his poo right on top of me as I was walking near the seaside. I was in my blonde phase at the time, so my daughter brightly said, 'At least it covers up your dark roots.' Very helpful!

I've seen numerous other people have their filled rolls, sandwiches and chips taken by these greedy thieves, so seagulls are my least favourite birds.

It always makes me think of how my mother highly disapproved of us eating outside other than at a proper picnic because she thought it looked common. Maybe she did have a point, if not for that reason. I wonder what she would think of everyone eating on the go now.

My Greatest Fear by Jacqueline Ellis

Born at the end of the Second World War,
I fear that a Third is already in store.
Salem is set on a hill far away.
Peace' is its name, but eludes it today.
"Peace" or "Shalom" is the greeting for Jews.
"Salamun alaykum" for Arabs. That's news!
Ishmael and Isaac have never made friends
And done what the God of their fathers intends.
Christ sent his disciples to spread the good word
That peace and forgiveness are far from absurd.
But two thousand years have elapsed, and it's late.
Why hasn't his message replaced war and hate?
The Nazis were guilty of great ethnic cleansing.
But Gaza's no different, it's no use pretending
Bombs raining down, and incredible sorrow
Can't be the answer for the world of tomorrow.
Where are the peacemakers? Have they all fled?
Will no one speak peace before we're all dead?
We need to stand up for a world of "Shalom",
And not for a world of the drone and the bomb!

What was I Afraid of? by Doug Dunn

It's Thursday 4th of July and I am travelling by steam train in North Wales with my son Lawrence. He booked us a return trip from Blaenau Ffestiniog to Porthmadog; a scenic eleven-mile journey by the narrow-gauge rail that once was used to transport slate from quarries and mines to the port.

In the souvenir guide I bought on the train; it says originally the train ran by gravity including high sided 'Dandy' wagons for horses to pull the empty wagons back up the line. Porthmadog, it says, did not exist before slate mining began in the 1830s.

My son lives in Manchester, and I felt happy that we arranged a short holiday fairly close to Snowdonia. It was good that the cottage we booked was of historic interest, right next to the steam railway. And yet, I also felt afraid of what was to come on the last day of our holiday. Lawrence said we could decide on the day, after checking out, whether to climb the whole way up or just drive through. We planned to visit and possibly climb up Snowdon.

When I was a child on a school outing, I remember feeling afraid of climbing Snowdon. The peak that lay ahead seemed so high up. For one reason or another, we were offered the choice of continuing up or going back down for an afternoon on the beach. I took the easy option but later regretted not seeing the views from the top.

When Friday morning came, I was still feeling afraid but pleased to see it was sunny and clear. We enjoyed a cooked breakfast and made packed lunches.

When we arrived at the Park and Ride we had to decide which route to take. We chatted with a group of hikers on the bus and decided to take the easier and more scenic; Mines' Track'.

We followed a path at the side of a lake and then the mountain peak appeared ahead. It was a little daunting. After three hours of walking and climbing including a stop for lunch we finally made it to the top.

The views were indeed breathtaking! With binoculars, we could see Porthmadog and the rail causeway we had walked along the day before. I felt pleased that we pressed on to the top.

The down journey was tricky in parts, but we took care not to slip on the stones. When we looked back at the summit, we saw thick clouds and realised it was our lucky day having such clear sunny skies.

A Memory by June Weeks

I grew up in a small, quiet farming village and was aged three when the 2nd World War was declared. In those early years, this had no significance for me and my little life went on as usual.

As I got a bit older, I remember certain words and phrases which lodged in my memory-Spitfires, enemy, explosions, doodle bugs, and I began to relate these words to being scared and fearful.

One day, I must have been about five, I was playing by myself in the lane outside our cottage when, suddenly, a squadron of aircraft swooped low over the village. I remember the noise as the planes screamed overhead and was literally rooted to the spot with terror. Then suddenly, I was scooped up and taken into shelter by a farmhand who was working nearby.

I was told, in later years, by my mother that, for a while, I became very quiet and jumpy but, thankfully, I adapted, as children do, to life's new experiences.

I never found out the nationality of those planes. Nevertheless, to this day, I feel a frisson of fear when low flying aircraft race by overhead.

Being Cast Adrift by Nolan Clarke

The year was 1953. I was thirteen plus years old and on holiday near the village of Flushing with two fifteen-year-old schoolgirls who lived nearby. Maureen had her own rowboat and crossed the river daily for schooling at Falmouth Grammar. Her friend, Margaret was my cousin who had been telling Maureen of her schoolboy cousin from Plymouth, who also had his own sailboat.

Together they had devised a fun test involving the removal of oars from the boat before casting Nolan adrift while they went to fetch ice creams. I heard them laughing as they walked up the beach, vowing to take their time and see how I would cope.

You may be thinking was I rescued? Had any other person observed my plight? The answers are No and Yes (by a very formidable character).

Searching for a means of propulsion I found that hands over the side would not do. Sitting perched on the stern (back end) and using my legs in a swimming mode would not do. My anger was rising, but that also would not do.

Searching the boat, I found a handheld water bailer and with contortions made slow movement towards the beach, but it was taking too long, and I was tiring. Then I had a light bulb moment. Why don't I use a floorboard? Yes, it made a passable paddle.

Arriving tired and vowing revenge, I espied the girls, their faces dripping ice cream, coming down the beach followed by an angry boatman.

'What have you done to my daughter's rowboat and where are the oars? And who are you boy?'

Margaret summed up the situation.

'He is my cousin, Nolan. Maureen and I were testing out his boat skills. He has his own sailboat back in Plymouth. We had been over to Falmouth.'

Mr Boatman summed up by saying, 'I don't know which of you girls was the stupidest or whether you, Nolan, was so naïve as to let two fifteen-year-old girls fake you on a trip. But we had better go to the house for refreshments and you can tell me about your boat in Plymouth. Also, I am keen to know how your mother is keeping. You will not know this, but she and I were school friends before the war. I was sorry when she went off with a fellow from up country. Your Ric---s family contributed so much to this area. I'm not surprised you are attracted to this area but watch these local girls.'

Writing for Pleasure Book 2

Tracey Troopers

Tracey Troopers by Helen Cowell

One day after visiting a local carnival, my daughter Heidi said she would like to become a majorette and take part in carnivals.

We searched around and visited local troupes, but didn't find any we liked. When talking to a friend, she said, "Why don't you start your own troupe?"

I thought it would be a good idea, but I would need some help. She then suggested her next door neighbour who was a music and games teacher at a public school. I went to meet her, and she agreed to help, and The Tracey Troopers were born.

Our first get together was in the Baptist Church. Heidi had asked many of her friends to come along on a Saturday morning. About twenty girls came. We then had to decide what we were going to do.

After a discussion we decided to do a pompom routine for local carnivals. We chose red and white as our team colours.

Now a dressmaker had to be found. A local lady offered to make them.

Red and white satin dresses were chosen with a pill box hat, white plimsolls and white socks. We now needed pompoms, so the parents got together around our snooker table and made them from red and white crepe paper. It was a very hard job with lots of blisters on the fingers, but it was worth it as they looked better than the shop ones.

Now before we could: go out and perform, we had to have a name. The girls were asked to think of a name and The Tracey Troopers was chosen. It was suggested by one of the parents, Anne Heydon.

Music was our next problem. We had a car to lead the troupe, but how were we going to play the music? A small trailer was obtained, and a tape recorder was put in the trailer with a generator and fixed to the car. A local businessman, Alan Clements, offered to use his car with proper equipment and loudspeakers on the top of the car and a large board with our name on it. We toured all the local carnivals and won a few prizes. The girls were now keen to enter competitions.

The following year we took part in our first competition at The Lord Mayors Day in Plymouth and to our delight we won first prize. We were so excited and now had an appetite to work hard and enter more competitions.

In October that year we decided to enter the Exeter Carnival. We booked our coach and off we went.

We all lined up for the start of the parade. There were many troupes taking part, all looking very smart in their uniforms.

Just before the carnival started, the heavens opened and down came the rain. We all started off on the parade. All the other troupes gave up one by one. We were the only troupe left, and Brenda, our trainer insisted we finished the route. Well, you can imagine what we looked like at the end of the carnival Our red dresses were so wet the red had run into the white. The hats had disintegrated as their base was only cardboard and the pompoms were no more as they were made from crepe paper.

We now had to have a new uniform we couldn't find a dressmaker locally so had to go to Bristol. The lady came down and measured all the girls. We still kept our red and white theme. There were a few problems along the way, but finally the day came for me to drive up and collect them.

On the way home I was driving in the fast lane on the motorway and my tyre burst! What a frightening experience. I had to cross three lanes of traffic and find a phone, no mobiles then. The police came out and changed the tyre. They were very helpful. I then had to find a telephone box in a nearby town to ring the parents to let them know I would be late getting back as the girls were practising and waiting for their uniforms as we were leaving early the next day for a competition.

The troupe ran for twenty-five years. I could write a whole book on our events, but it would become very boring so I -will try and give a potted version of those happy years.

As we became more confident in our performances we did baton twirling, and military routines and entered into solo performances.

We joined The British Baton Twirling Association and National Baton Twirling Association and travelled all over the country entering competitions and National Finals.

We were National Champions in many competitions and some of the girls were outstanding in the individual competitions and won many trophies. I will tell you about some of the exciting times we had.

In the 1980s we went to Jersey twice. The first time we took part in The Battle of Flowers Parade, it was magical, parading along the seafront on a beautiful summer's day with all the beautiful floats and walkers and the icing on the cake was winning first prize. We stayed there for several days in a hostel we slept in dormitories and had a rota of duties we had to perform every day. "We travelled there and back by ferry from Weymouth.

The second year we went we decided to go by hovercraft from Torquay as it was much quicker. That was a big mistake as the day we went was a rainy day even though it was August.

We all arrived at the pier to board the hovercraft. When we saw it we were shocked as it looked only fit for the scrap yard. However, we boarded along with other members of the public going on their holidays including Allen and Jacqui. I didn't know he was going, and he didn't expect to see me there. The weather was still very bad with poor visibility and the sea was very choppy. It was so bad they didn't open the snack bars, and it was rolling from side to side. Most of the passengers were poorly. Our seats were on the lower deck. We could see the fish swimming by, and the water started coming in and all the luggage that was on the floor was very wet.

When we arrived near St Helier, we couldn't dock because of the weather conditions, so we had to keep circling around until we had the all clear. It was a very frightening experience. We were all dreading the return journey when we were told our hovercraft had been taken back to Torquay and scrapped at Dartmouth and we returned home on a lovely sunny day by a very nice ferry to Weymouth.

Forty

The year of 1984 by Linda Corkerton

In the year of nineteen eighty -four,

In the town of Bovey Tracey, gateway to the moor,

The elders stirred from contemplation and took the lead,

Creating an activity trust to meet their needs,

Not knowing if their venture would succeed.

In the year of nineteen eighty -four,

Images of miners, boots and hooves into living rooms roll,

Whilst local lorries deliver sacks of coal.

Across the newsagent's counter the news was sold,

Print ink on fingertips, no smartphone in hand, the bad news tolled.

Streaming, podcasts and 24hour news were yet to unfold.

In the year of nineteen eighty -four.

Seven pubs opened their doors,

Cash on counters, no bank card in hand,

A pint of bitter and the occasional band.

No baristas, ground coffee or flat whites

But conversation and banter into the night.

In the year of twenty twenty-four

The high street now has different doors,

Gone are the banks, some pubs are no more.

The hospital no longer provides for the town,

But proud stands the distillery in the town hall surrounds,

And creative arts, in so many forms, abound.

In the year of twenty twenty-four,

The book shop, long gone, came back anew,

Whilst the library and council made a move, long overdue.

The trust now thrives in its purpose-built home

With solar panels and Wi-Fi, terms little known,

In the year of nineteen eighty-four.

Forty by Brenda Heale

When I was very young

and my house was very cold

I had ice inside the windows

and chilblains on my toes

and I always thought that Forty

was very very old.

Now I am old myself

my house is warm and cosy

Thanks to the central heating

So no chilblains on my toesies

The only trouble is that the bills are not much fun

and now I think that Forty

is very, very young.

Forty Years on by Maria Kinnersley

'Here, Jon, grab hold of that wiring, will you?'
'Why Me? I'm busy.'

'Doing what? Drop that sheet of paper you're wandering around with and come here.'

'Come on then. What do you want me to do?'

'Just hold onto to this while I fix the other end. The rate I'm going, I'm never going to be ready for the Talent Show.'

'It's exciting, isn't it? Eighty years! Who would have thought BTAT would have lasted so long? It's strange to think, my mum and dad were members and, in the talent show in 2024, and now I'm involved. I bet if they were here now, they would see many changes,'

'Give us the wire you're holding now, Jon. Great. Now it's sorted. We'll be able to see Minnie now when she does her Moon dance. That wouldn't have happened forty years ago. Just think. I was looking at the records last night. Forty years ago, the hall only seated seventy. Now there's room for seven hundred.'

'Yes, and next year they're talking about limiting the age of joining to eighty because people are so healthy and living much longer. You should see the waiting list. Look at Minnie – Ninety years old and on holiday on the Moon.'

'And we're going to see Sara as well – you know – the one living on Mars now. She's doing an acrobatic number. I don't want to miss that. You're looking thoughtful, Jon.'

'I wonder how they would celebrate in another forty years. That'll be 2104.'

'Well however they do it, son, I'm sure it will be in true BTAT fashion.'

The 'Forties' by Peter Debnam

In March 1945, my mum, who had been told she would be unlikely to conceive again – I have a sister born in 1938 – became pregnant again. She was so overjoyed – well, who wouldn't be with little ole me on the way- that on the day she got the news, Semyon Timoshenko a Russian General broke through on the Eastern Front to capture Vienna from the German Army, so she thought that would be the name for me! But my Father was not really enamoured with this name, so my Russian name which sounded very grand was never adopted. I simply became 'Peter'!

As the world emerged before me, my first memory is still retained as it was so traumatic no doubt.

There I was sitting in my pram being taken down a steep hill in St Budeaux in Plymouth, when my mother slipped. I can see now the gathering momentum before me and wondered if I was to survive the day, when a face and arm appeared at my side and very gradually, I was brought to a halt. Everything happened like a slow-motion event, but I survived!

At the very end of the Forties, I started school, and I recall entering my first classroom and being shown an incredible sandpit with all sorts of building pieces and dinky toy vehicles. I immediately set forth on making roads and houses accompanied by a very pretty girl with long black hair wearing a pleated skirt. When a lad tried to mess up what we'd done, I pushed him away: he fell over, and I was immediately in big trouble! Was this early defence of the fairer sex an unconscious part of my make up. I don't really know!

But I do know, some things never change!!!

Rainy Days by Ann Turner

Rain, rain please go away.

But I know you'll be back another day.

15th of July, it's meant to be summer!

Thirty-nine more like this? What a bummer.

If I eat an apple, as I should on this day.
Will you please make the rain go away.

I have on my wellies, I have on my coat.
But at this rate, will I need a small boat?

Rain, rain please go away.
It's BTAT's Fortieth birthday and we want to play!

Forty by Jane Newman

"Life begins at forty" said so often when people reach that particular age, and, yes, we do seem to explore and travel and investigate perhaps that little bit more in our forties. We first went skiing then and visits to far flung continents and many historical sites weren't visited until we were gone forty.

However, on reflection our children and grandchildren did all this well before they were forty so that comparison doesn't really apply anymore, but whichever way we look at it we cannot enjoy life after forty without the input that occurred during the previous forty years.

Right from the beginning, from conception, what we will be doing in our later years is the result of nursing, nurturing, clothing, teaching, caring, planning and guiding, not just from one's parents, and grandparents, but from the many, many, people taking part in our development.

Just after I began to think about this theme for the subject, 'Forty', I heard Mike Watson's splendid talk about BTAT's history; I realised that the fact that celebrating being forty couldn't happen without the input of what went before also applied to this wonderful organisation.

Forty years ago it was conceived, people coming together with an idea. These were the people that fed and nurtured us, BTAT, watching us grow. They helped and planned our reconstruction and made sure we were healthy and sound and would last for more generations to enjoy. Then came their offspring if you like, and their friends. They moved us forward with modern technology to protect and ensure, and insure, that this building, always bright, warm and welcoming, is still here for people to enjoy as they grow older.

Thank you BTAT and your many ancestors that aren't with us anymore. I am, personally, so glad that you are here.

Musings on '40' by Jane Shann

40 – Marriage, fun, love, laughter.

40 – Children, parties, broken sleep.

40 - Teenagers, angst, break up, sorrow. Are they safe?

40 – Empty nest syndrome. My life was them, my identity intermingled. It is lost.

40 – He wants a promotion, more money, more prestige. Golf. I hate golf.

40 – It's half of 80.

40 – Rethink, reframe, rephrase.

40 – Divorce

40 – What is my purpose? Why am I here?

40 – I am asleep.

40

Musings over, it's time to go

I look in the mirror and put on a smile.

To celebrate the years that BTAT's grown

How many of these, it now? Ah yes!

40

Writing for Pleasure Book 2

What Matters

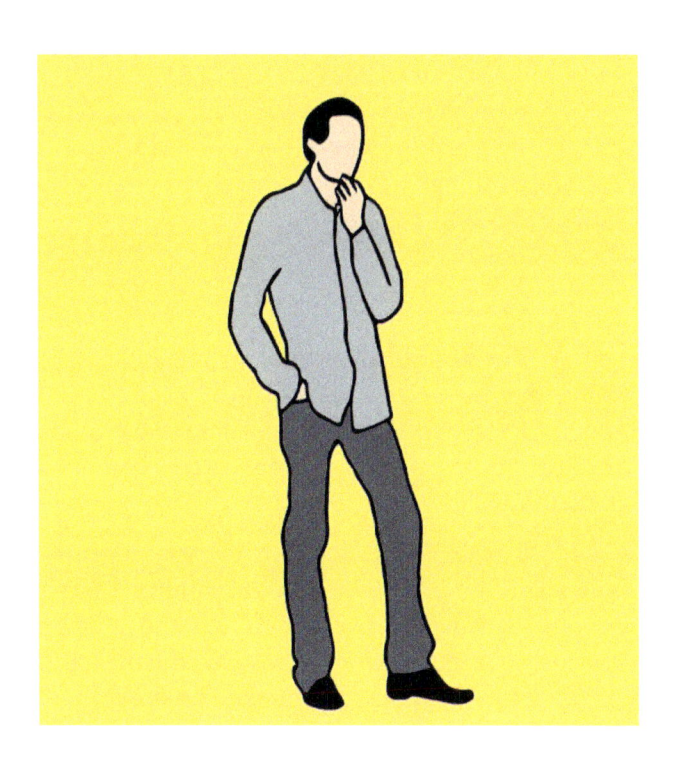

Resolutions by Arnold Sharpe

The New Year is a fine time to reflect on what matters to yourself and in your life. It's a time to make up for your inadequacies during the previous year. In a word, to make New Year's resolutions.

For the most part New Year's resolutions are admissions of previous failures. A thing or things you have not carried out. Take for example the resolution, I must be a nicer person.

Doomed to failure from the outset.

The same applies to many resolutions. I will finish that decorating job! I will lose weight! I will cut out the chocolate! I will cut the lawn more often! I will concentrate on the garden! I will be nice to my wife!

Research has shown that ninety percent of resolutions fall by the wayside within a month. This means that by February the resolutory (is that a word?); anyway, the maker of resolutions, is back to where he or she or that person was before Christmas.

Now let us take a closer look. Let's say that I resolved to be a nastier person. By February research says I will probably have failed. Will this mean that I will have become a nicer person? I doubt it.

In a lot of the other resolutions this negative resolve could be an unrivalled success. I will not do any decorating! I will let the garden grow wild! The dogs can go to the dogs! I will not be nice to my wife! (I must warn my readers this particular resolution can have very dangerous consequences).

If, as research tells us, all my resolutions resulted in failure. Come February I will be in my garden, the lawn mower will have sharpened blades and after I have walked the dogs, I will be ready to paint the back bedroom. Whether my wife will be smiling at me, now that is always open to question.

So, the moral of this story could be, each New Year have no resolutions no goals. This will lead to contentment and fewer disappointments. Which surely will lead to a more successful New Year.

What Matters by Peter Debnam

I ask myself 'What does matter to me as I pass through the autumn of my years'. (A Frank Sinatra number by the way).

Well, King Charles summed it up in his Christmas Day speech when he wished that 'the power of light overcoming darkness is celebrated across the boundaries of faith and belief'. I would like that light to overcome every issue, both worldwide and in my own personal life, the latter of which I can do something about.

To me, light in an active and real sense is interpreted as expressing love in every situation I find myself in, including those situations where so often because we are human, we take an opposing position. I am reminded of the life of Merlin Carothers, an American forces pastor who took praising God in every situation to a whole new level. He would praise and thank God for the most difficult and seemingly negative situations in both his life and that of members of his family and flock; incredibly the situations always turned around for good. Essentially, he let the 'light' into every situation. His argument was that bad issues were part of one's existence but should ALWAYS be addressed by a loving and positive response. The best recent example of this was the former Plymouth Royal Marine, Mark Ormrod who lost both his legs and his right arm in an Afghanistan bomb blast, yet on Christmas Eve may have won the world record for the fastest triple amputee 1km swim!

There will be very few events – if any - as difficult as Mark's, so, in 2023 I challenge each one of us when faced with 'What Matters' in our own lives to 'let the light in' and so overcome any personal darkness in our thoughts and actions.

Writing for Pleasure Book 2

All I Want for Christmas…

Christmas Memories by June Weeks

The build-up to Christmas never started until December. Money was short, everything was rationed but mum made sure my brother and I had a magical time. She made every part of the preparations so exciting, starting with the decorations, stored in a battered suitcase under the bed - old homemade paper chains, baldish tinsel and folding paper bells.

An afternoon was selected to put up the decorations, teetering on chairs, with drawing pins to loop the chains to the beams.

Huge excitement when dad brought home the tree - placed in a bucket swathed in red crepe paper. Again, a special time would be selected to adorn the branches with homemade ornaments, tinsel and real candles in metal clip on holders and the star placed ceremoniously on the top. I can vividly remember mum lighting the candles, turning off the lights and we would stand there bathed in the soft flickering light - magical!

Well wrapped up, we would take a walk to where the best holly (with plenty of berries) grew and take home sprigs which were then tucked above the mirror and every picture.

Our entertainment was by way of the bulky temperamental 'wireless' on which 'expert' dad would eventually find the correct station for the news and children's programmes.

Writing letters to Santa, church bells and carol singers were all part of the excitement and, on Christmas morning, after exploring the knobbly socks at the end of our beds, we would creep downstairs to find a pile of presents for both of us - very modest by today's standards but always what we wished for.

Each Christmas through my childhood was simple, particularly compared to the mercenary affair it has become but, thanks to my mum, was full of excitement, mystery and magic. All I want for Christmas is a return to those kinds of celebrations which always reflected its true meaning.

Christmas Past by Peter Duxbury

Christmas is to celebrate the return of the light. Firstly, let's return to the start of the year on the 31st of October when the sun god is sacrificed and travels to the underworld with his goddess. Through this embrace he is reborn as the child of light on Winter Solstice on the

21st of December. The Oak King from the Summer Solstice is reborn as the Holly King. Leaves that no longer serve have been released and there is a hope for new beginnings.

The Vikings decorated their Yule Log tree with wreaths of mistletoe, fir cones, holly berries and feathers. In England the tree was the oak, in Scotland the birch, in Devon the ash. Bringing the log indoors for twelve days to display or burn for warmth and light. The Christians took this over to subdue what they called pagan. And the French and Swiss took this over to become a chocolate covered Swiss roll for burning calories instead of smoky fires. Or perhaps we can have small fires on candles on the wooden Yule Log?

During the twelve-day festival children fill their boots with straw to leave out for the Norse god Odin. Odin is the gift-bearer soaring through the skies on his flying eight-legged white horse, Sleipnir, with sword-maiden Valkyries. Odin would slip down chimneys and deliver toys to the waiting children's boots. Odin was forbidden by the Christians and replaced by the fourth-century Greek bishop Saint Nicholas. Eventually to be taken over in America by Santa Claus and the Coca Cola company to be dressed in red, and a time for commercialism.

Wouldn't it be nice to leave aside commercialism and return to the Green Man and our natural connection to the Earth? All I want for Christmas is for peace without the conflict of religions.

All I Want… by Brenda Heale

All I want for Christmas is…

For the wars to stop and the men with power to realise it's all a waste of time and to live peacefully. We can't bring back the dead but why keep killing and maiming?

For the children in Yemen who are scared and hungry to be given food and comfort.

For the homeless to have homes and jobs and to build new lives.

For the children of Africa to have food and education.

For girls all over the world to be given equal opportunities.

For the Uyghur Muslims in China to be treated properly.

For global warming to be taken seriously.

For the world to care.

Oh, and please, a nice big box of Chocolate Brazil's for me. Thanks.

What I Wish by Jean Newman

Three months ago, our great-granddaughter's baby brother arrived, so there were now two little people to become part of our family.

I had watched their grandpa, and then their daddy, grow to adulthood with lots of tears and laughter along the way; there have been many happy birthdays, seaside holidays, family gatherings, celebrations, days out, train rides, bus rides, car rides, a myriad of happenings to linger in the memory.

But I won't experience this whole transition with these two new little people. Hopefully, maybe, I'll see them off to school, run an egg-and-spoon race, learn to swim, ride a bike, but what will the world that they join in later life, be like? I wish I knew; I want to know; I want to be there.

So, what has this to do with what I wish for Christmas? It's hard to define. It can't be wrapped in special paper, with labels and bows. It's a vision I suppose. So, I wish for Christmas that they will still find the world a very special place, that the seasons will stay the same, that the sun will shine on a summer mornings, the frost sparkle in the winter months and that they will chase the autumn leaves and build snowmen, and paddle in puddles.

I hope that the winds will stay soft to caress, not destroy, that the rain will freshen our rivers, and keep the countryside green, not flood our homes and ravage our cities. I wish, and hope, that technology won't prevent them from finding joy in listening to a blackbird singing after rain, or delight in watching a robin nearby as they dig in the garden or watch a thrush wash in a birdbath.

And I hope so much that they will find the world a happy place to be, that the troubled countries of today will no longer be in conflict, and that the simple things of life will give them pleasure, just as it did, and does, for me.

Friendship by Maria Kinnersley

Ronnie Rat was having a bad day. As he stomped away from the front door from the nth time today, he caught a fragment of the song being warbled by Dickie Bird on his tiny radio.

'All I want this Christmas is you...oo,' sang the bird.

'All I want this Christmas,' Ronnie shouted, 'is to be LEFT ALONE!!'

He sighed. He knew he was being unreasonable. His best friend Milo Mole had gone to visit his brother Max this Christmas.

'He hasn't been well,' explained Milo avoiding the look on Ronnie's stricken face. 'I thought I'd pay him a visit.

Meantime, the world and his wife seemed intent on visiting the sad rat.

First to come had been the Robin twins. Then Wensleigh Weasel turned up followed by Fred and Freda the fieldmice. When Tommy Thrush had pecked at the door, Ronnie gave up being polite.

'I want to be left alone,' he bawled at the bewildered bird. 'Tell everyone to leave me alone.'

He burrowed into his chair and put his head under the fat red cushion there. So, he didn't hear the gentle tap at the door. A few minutes later, Ronnie's mobile phone rang.

Muttering under his breath, he swiped up and roared, 'What?'

'It's Milo,' said a familiar voice. 'Open the door.'

'But you're not here,' said the rat.

'Max wanted to come to see you. He said all his best Christmases with you have been the best because you're so friendly.' The voice paused. 'Or have you changed?'

Ronnie scampered to the door and opened it. There in front of him was Milo with his brother, Max. But behind were all the woodland creatures each with a parcel of food and drink.

Ronnie swallowed. 'I've been very selfish,' he said, looking down at his plush carpet. 'I shouldn't have remembered that we are all friends, and you all were trying to keep me company. I'm sorry. Come on in.'

And they all had the best Christmas ever.

Christmas by Jacqueline Ellis

At Christmas, as I quaff my wine,
I wish the day to turn out fine,
That all the clan, those kids of mine,
Will stop their quarrels, fall in line
And round the table laugh and dine
Instead of causing me to pine!

At Christmas, while the candles burn,
All human heart, again they yearn
For peace on Earth, and then they turn
And see the wars, and so they spurn
The very season they should learn
That love, not war, must now return.

The End

Printed in Great Britain
by Amazon